SIX OF THE
BEST
EROTIC
GAY
STORIES

SIX OF THE BEST
EROTIC
GAY
STORIES

Kenny Dima

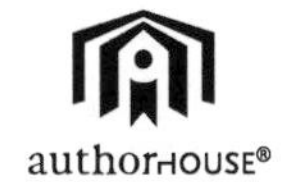

authorHOUSE®

AuthorHouse™ UK Ltd.
1663 Liberty Drive
Bloomington, IN 47403 USA
www.authorhouse.co.uk
Phone: 0800.197.4150

Published by AuthorHouse   07/15/2013

ISBN: 978-1-4817-6995-2 (sc)
ISBN: 978-1-4817-6996-9 (e)

THE SLAVE GAME

Chapter 1

SAYING GOODBYE TO MUM and dad was a lot easier than I imagined. Apart from holidays I'd never been away from home and felt really grown up; I waved goodbye to them again through the window of the train as it eased out of the station. The feeling of excitement and apprehension mingled together as I tried to visualise in my mind what the first day at university would be like. I'd never been a good mixer at school or college probably because I knew I was different; surely there were other guys out there who preferred boys to girls!

I didn't remember dropping off but when I woke the carriage was full. The handsome man sitting opposite smiled and with his eyes signalled a message for me to look down towards my crotch—I had a hard-on and the Great Pyramid of Egypt was there for everyone to see! I nervously placed my hands over the display and felt the blood rush to my face with embarrassment then closed my eyes. When I opened them again I saw the blond-haired man who had alerted me to my humiliation smiling and I thought 'what the heck' I'm not likely to see anyone on this train in the near future and returned his happy gaze.

His hypnotising stare locked with mine, filling my thoughts with a desire I'd never felt before. For a brief moment I was distracted as the train came to a halt and many commuters alighted leaving the smiling stranger and myself alone in the compartment but when I glanced back he had unzipped his jeans and was holding his uncut erection with both hands. I stared in disbelief at the beautiful flesh just inches away from my face; I wanted—no, needed to taste the pink skin peeking from his fist. I looked up with bulging eyes to his face and he nodded his consent. An instant later I was on my knees gorging on the luscious post, listening to his panting over the clatter of the train's wheels, I built up a rhythm with my lips then ran my left hand up inside his T-shirt touching hairy skin; he sighed loudly. With my other hand I swiftly took out my cock and began pulling to and fro. Hands gripped either side of my head forcing me down harder, deeper and faster. I was bobbing up and down as fast as the wheels were going round when a voice above me shouted a warning, "I'm coming!"

I thrust his hot pole as deep into my mouth as I could, my nose nudging the silky soft pubic hair and then the exploding fountain of sperm hit my throat; that was all the encouragement I needed to shoot my own sperm across the carriage floor. The flesh wedged in my face began to wilt and I slowly lifted myself off the magnificent cock, the hands that had gripped my head so tightly now gently caressed my cropped hair. I stuffed my depleted cock back into my trousers before standing up then looked down onto the smiling man's handsome face. "My name's Jack." He held out a hand.

"And I'm Martin." I rubbed my hand on my trousers before making contact in case I'd left anything sticky on it!

Jack stood up and adjusted his clothing as the train pulled into a station, he must have seen the disappointed look in my eyes and laughed.

"I'm not getting off yet, I'm going all the way to Vale, the university stop!"

"But that's where I'm going, Vale University!" I said excitedly. "It's my first time and I may need some help finding my way around."

"Have you somewhere to stay?"

"No, but I've been given a list of addresses of people who accommodate students."

"Yes, and no doubt the rooms will be infested with cockroaches and let the water in when it rains," he smiled, "I think it may be a good idea if you bunk in with me, after all we do have something in common, don't we?" He winked.

"Gee, thanks Jack; that would be great!"

On reaching our destination we struggled with our heavy baggage out of the station to a waiting taxi, five minutes later the cab stopped on a tree lined avenue in a very elegant part of town.

"You live here?" I asked stupidly.

"My aging father has property all over the country; he lets me use this place while I'm at Vale. Here, let me give you a hand with that bag, it looks heavy." He picked it up as if it weighed nothing.

"You must work-out a lot." I studied his broad shoulders while he lifted the holdall.

"A couple of times a week, there's a gym in the basement."

He opened the door and I was in another world. The word opulence came to mind as I took in the elegant hallway leading to the wide, curved staircase.

"Come on, I'll show you your room."

We climbed the stairs then passed many doors before stopping at the one marked 'guestroom'. He switched on the light and I gasped! The room was blue, every shade imaginable, the ceiling, walls, deep piled carpet, even the massive bed. Erotic pictures of naked men hung on the walls as did a huge plasma television. It was fantastic, but . . .

"Look, Jack, thanks for offering me a room but the allowance I've got won't cover the cost of a place like this."

"Let's not talk about that now, Martin. University doesn't start for first year students for another week, we'll find some way for you to pay your share. Do you like Chinese? I'll phone an order through, I'm starving."

I began unpacking my bag and heard Jack talking on the telephone.

"Get yourself showered; the food will be here in ten minutes." Jack shouted from a long way off.

The shower room was as luxurious as the bedroom, an assortment of gels and shampoos tidily arranged on a shelf. I stripped out of my clothes and saw my image in the full length mirror occupying the whole wall, I vainly watched myself do a series of exercises; I had a good size chest and narrow waist, my suntan had recently been topped up during a heat wave and the only body hair was around my bits! I smiled at myself; tonight I looked and felt on top of the world. I stepped into the shower, adjusted the heat then removed the cap from a bottle and sniffed the liquid; the pungent aroma hit my nostrils like smelling salts. The sweet perfume was nothing like I'd ever smelled before and although I was feeling dizzy I poured some of the gel into my hands and smothered my body in the unusual foam; I was on cloud nine!

"There's something for you to wear on the chair outside." Jack's voice startled me as I rinsed the heady fragrance from my body. After towelling myself dry

I stepped into the blue bedroom; over the back of an armchair was a colourful Kimono, there were no other clothes in the room; all of my stuff had disappeared! I dressed in the silky material and noted it must have been made for someone with very short legs; it barely covered my bum!

"You look very sexy!"

I turned at the speed of light to see Jack standing at the door with a wide grin on his handsome face. He was wearing an identical robe.

"Come on, the food's getting cold." I followed him down the stairs and into the dining room; more lavishness greeted me, a huge chandelier hung over the long wooden table surrounded by six high backed chairs; we sat next to each other at one end. Jack served the meal from polystyrene dishes equally onto two china plates; there was far too much. A bottle of chilled white wine was taken from an ice bucket and poured into crystal glasses. "Cheers! Here's to a lasting friendship."

"Cheers and thanks, Jack, for what you've done."

"I never thanked *you* Martin, for what you did on the train," we both laughed, "tell me something about yourself." He asked while piling his plate with more yellow rice.

"I'm eighteen, live with mum and dad, bit of a loner really, you know, not many friends."

"You must have someone to practice on; you gave me the best blow job ever."

"I've never done it to anybody before, it just came naturally."

"Are you telling me you've never had a relationship?"

"That's right, I suppose I'm a bit shy—well, I was until today!" More laughter.

After the meal, the empty dishes were scooped up and disposed of, I offered to do the washing up but Jack said it would be taken care of later. We moved to the brightly lit lounge and sat together on a wide leather settee. He rested a warm hand on my thigh and I felt a twinge in my sack followed by a movement inside my gown. I tried to close my legs together but Jack's hand slid down and seized my rising stem. "Relax, you've seen mine, why shouldn't I see yours!" he whispered.

He pulled the flimsy material open and I took in a deep breath as a hand stroked my stomach and chest gently tweaking one nipple and then the other. Although my eyes were shut I sensed his face was close; I felt his lips touch mine. I responded as best I could, this was the first time for me. While still kissing, he removed my Kimono and laid me down, all the while touching and feeling the most sensitive parts of my body; I was in paradise!

He slowly kissed my neck, then my chest, moving gradually down my stomach until he reached my pulsating cock. "Ahhh!" I heard myself cry out as he began licking the underside of my crown, and then his lips engulfed the entire column in one rapid movement. I grabbed his head to make him stay still, I was sure I would come if he moved. The exploring tongue flicked over the sensitive skin as his head slowly returned to my helmet driving me into an uncontrollable frenzy. My legs jerked with pleasure and I began digging my fingernails into his back as the head of steam began building up. Jack must have sensed my imminent eruption; he moved from cock to balls, nibbling gently on the delicate skin before taking one ball in his mouth and then the other and all the time his gentle hands were roaming over my body. A hand went between my thighs and began searching, moving fingers tantalised around my hole and then something was inside me; a finger was probing my inside! I thought I had experienced the best of the best already with Jack but this new sensation was stimulating me beyond my wildest dreams! I felt the exploring digit touch something deep within me and I couldn't hold back any longer.

"Oh, Jack! I'm coming! I'm coming!" I yelled and clamped my arse cheeks together trapping his finger inside as the first of many jets flew high into the air. I lay exhausted on the settee.

"You're the first person I've met who can come without jerking off." Jack smiled while using the remote control to operate some electronic gadget.

"Nothing like that has ever happened to me before. I can't believe what I've been missing."

"Let's freshen up." He squeezed my shoulder. The shower next to the lounge reminded me of the one in the sports hall at college. It was long enough to clean twenty bodies at the same time.

"Wow! Why is it so big?"

"The previous owner did everything on a grand scale." He said in a matter-of-fact manner.

Jack's body was powerful, just turning the tap on made his muscles flex; he caught me watching him in the mirror and smiled.

"Let me wash your back, Martin." I moved closer under the cascading water and felt strong hands rub the same perfumed gel into my skin as I'd used earlier. I became light headed as before.

"What is this stuff? It makes me feel woozy."

"It's a special deep cleansing lotion, don't you like it?"

Jack stood behind me, his soapy hands around my body moving in circles and gradually dropping lower until the inevitable happened. The gel had me hard in an instant and the slow to and fro action along with the sweet aroma excited me beyond belief. I was aware something was pressing hard against my hole and I was a little frightened; a finger was one thing but the enormous size of Jack's cock was another.

"Why don't you let me take you to bed, I'll be very gentle with you." He whispered in my ear.

"I don't know, Jack. You're twice as big as me in that department."

"I've got some special cream; you won't even know I'm there!"

I had always wanted to experience the feeling but now it was going to happen I was a little scared. I dried and with trepidation followed him to my blue-room.

"Where's my stuff?" I remembered it had gone missing while I showered earlier.

"All your clothes are in the laundry and your books are safely put away." He tapped my bum, urging me forward towards the bed. He worked himself up and stretched a condom over his massive cock, then from under the pillow, removed a tube and unscrewed the cap.

"This is not going to hurt, is it?"

"Not if you completely relax." He assured me. Bright lights suddenly filled the room and I became agitated. "Nothing to worry about, I just like to see what I'm doing."

He positioned me on my side with my legs bent and began smearing some cool creamy stuff up and around my hole; the light touch of soothing fingers stimulated my cock again and a moment later I felt the tip of his cock slide up and down, searching for the entry point.

"Just relax and think of what we did earlier."

The wedge had located the gap and was pushing very slowly forward, as if asking the hole to widen. He withdrew slightly then pushed forward a little harder. I felt the head slip inside me, gradually moving in and out, each gentle thrust going deeper. I didn't make a sound, not a murmur passed my lips, I began wanking myself, enjoying the moment, then I felt his skin touch mine and I knew he was all the way in. The rhythm began, slowly at first but gathering speed all the time. In the back of my mind I could hear the clattering of the train's wheels and almost smiled. Jack began puffing, he must be reaching his climax, I thought. I squeezed my cheeks tightly together; I was on the brink of coming myself, my balls tightened, I couldn't hold back any longer. I moaned loudly and tried to catch the stuff in my hand but it was going everywhere.

"Was I OK, Jack?" He had stopped moving, probably exhausted from his evening of passion. I eased myself forward and off his probe; when I looked back Jack's eyes were closed and he was not moving. "Jack? What's wrong?"

My heart began racing and I was really scared. I shook my new friend but he didn't respond. Jack was dead!

I heard a sound like a door closing and raced along the landing then remembered I was naked. I made myself as small as possible at the top of the staircase and listened to someone moving about.

"Where are you, Jack? I know you're home, you've left every damn light on in the house, it looks like a Christmas tree from outside!" A harsh voice called. "Jesus Christ, look at this mess. You can clear this up before you go to bed. Jack, I'm talking to you! Why the hell don't you answer me?"

The angriness of the newcomer's tone began to frighten me, I was under the impression Jack lived alone.

"Jack, I'm going to take a shower, be a love and get me a drink, I've had a pig of a day!" There was a touch of tenderness in the voice and as soon as I heard the sound of water running, I dashed down the stairs into the lounge, grabbed the Kimono and onwards towards the front door; then stopped! Where could I go? I've neither clothes nor money. Jack had stowed all my possessions away for some reason. If I went to the police what could I tell them and what if Jack didn't die from natural causes, what if he had been poisoned? The water in the shower stopped flowing and I saw through the partially open door the man drying himself. I stood still in the hallway waiting for the door to open fully. When it did a naked man of about forty-something stood staring at me.

We looked at each other open-mouthed neither of us knowing what to say first.

"You're wearing my Kimono!" He seemed more concerned about the garment than who I was and what I was doing in this house.

"I'm Martin; Jack invited me back for a meal!" What else could I say; he brought me back to fuck my arse?

"You can call me Mike. Where's Jack now, sleeping it off, I suppose!"

"He didn't look well; he's lying on the bed in the guest room." Not really a lie, very close to the truth in fact.

"In the lounge you'll find a decanter full of brandy and some glasses, pour me a large one while I wake the sleeping beauty." He smiled.

I poured two glasses while waiting for the scream or whatever people do when they find somebody lifeless.

The man was actually smiling when he entered the room and took the crystal glass from my hand. "He's dead to the world! Cheers."

I almost choked at hearing those words, how could anyone be so callous?

"I'm sorry for your loss, he was fine one minute and gone the next." I waited for some reaction.

He began laughing, not a chuckle but a full belly laugh. "Jack suffers from a sleeping disorder or to be precise a stay-awake disorder. Too much excitement sends him off in seconds and as he's still wearing a condom I think I know what may have caused the problem tonight." He reached forward, put his hand under the Kimono and gently squeezed my cock.

He must have seen the worry drain from my face as he began laughing again. "Come, sit beside me and tell me how you got here."

We sat in the same place where Jack and me had performed earlier. As I recited the meeting on the train, he wanted every detail of the blow job, even of me wanking myself and before I'd finished the story he lifted my hand and placed it on his rock-hard cock. "Tell me again I'm sure you must have left something out!" He was panting as my hand raced up and down his circumcised cock, which was easily as big as Jack's. Mike's hand found my erection; a little goo had seeped out of the pee hole and he smeared it around my helmet driving me wild. I manoeuvred myself between his wide spread legs and, kneeling on the carpet, began sucking his lollypop. What started as a murmur soon turned into a loud moan and finally a yell as the stuff filled my mouth.

"Oh, my God! Where did you learn to do that with your tongue, it was fantastic!"

"That's funny, Jack said the same thing!" We both laughed. The glasses were replenished and we sat giggling over silly stories we each remembered from our childhood.

Mike picked up the TV remote control saying he wanted to watch the news but when the picture appeared there was no newsreader, just Jack and myself on the settee. Mike quickly grabbed the remote and switched to another station.

"I don't mind watching the film," I squeezed his powerful thigh, "I've never seen myself on television before." I didn't know Jack had been recording the night's entertainment on DVD. The cameras were set at different angles allowing the audience a complete panoramic view and I know it may sound conceited but I looked gorgeous! My cock looked bigger than I'd ever seen it before and when I came without touching myself we both said "wow" at the same time as streaks of come hit the ceiling.

"Did Jack leave the lights on when you did it upstairs?"

"Yes, why?"

"Because he probably recorded that as well!"

Neither of us heard him enter the room, a hand touched my head and probably Mike's then a voice shouted "Boo" causing both of us to jump six inches into the air. Jack laughed out loud. "What did you think of the premier? Will I get an Oscar for my performance?" He wanted to know.

"Maybe Martin will, he's got the most sensitive tongue in the world." Mike reckoned.

"You don't have to tell me. That was the most exciting train ride I've ever taken. Having this illness has its compensations you know, I'm not allowed to drive anymore so riding on public transport does have its pleasures."

"You frightened me, I thought you were dead." I chipped in when the laughter ceased.

"Don't you worry about me young man, there's plenty of spunk left in this old tube!" He waved his cock to and fro keeping the merriment going.

"Are you two a couple?" I was eager to know as much as I could about the gay world.

"Yes, you could say that. We've been together for several years and like most people we have our ups and downs. Why do you ask?" Jack smiled.

"I thought couples loved each other like my mum and dad."

The long silence was broken by Mike, "In the gay scene there are people who, like your mum and dad, stay together and never stray. But we like to spice up our life occasionally and although we love each other we're not jealous and share whoever walks through the door.

"So I'm not the first."

"Nor the last, hopefully," Jack smiled, "but that doesn't mean we can't remain friends. You have a lot to learn and over the next few days before you start at university perhaps you'll let us show you the ropes. That way you can choose what you like to do best, some people like to be dominant while others are passive. We'll give you a much better education than you'll ever get down the road."

"When do the lessons begin?" I was eager to learn.

"Now," Mike said sternly, "get yourself in the dining room and clear up that filthy mess you made earlier. Wash the plates and glasses and polish the dining table. You are our slave and you do as we say, understand?"

"Yes." I said timidly.

"I didn't hear you, louder!"

"Yes sir, I'll do it right away, sir."

"And another thing, you wear nothing inside this house, is that clear?" Jack shouted with fire in his eyes.

The change in their mood took me completely by surprise, I'd heard of schizophrenia but this must be the severest case known to man, however I complied with their orders and began cleaning the house. By midnight I was worn out and they gave me permission to go to bed. Jack's used condom was still on the sheet where he had discarded it. I threw it down the toilet then pissed on it! I adjusted the crumpled pillows and found the tube Jack had used earlier. The label read 'lubricating jelly' and I remembered what it felt like when spread around my hole. I squeezed a little into the palm of my hand and was just about to spread it along the length of my aroused cock when the door flew open.

"Oh no you don't! You are ours now and you don't pleasure yourself in any way without our permission." Jack shouted then snatched the fun stuff out of my hand. Mike entered, "Put these on, it'll stop you playing with yourself!"

"Boxing gloves? You've got to be kidding me!"

"Put them on, Slave Boy, do as you're told or you'll be sorry!" Jack's harshness was creepy. I pulled each of the gloves on and allowed Mike to tie them securely. When they left I looked at myself in the big bathroom mirror and took up the pose of a boxer, dancing and punching. "Go to bed, Slave Boy!" Came the order; they were watching me! I drank from the water bottle left beside the bed and slept.

Chapter 2

IT WAS DARK AND I wondered where I was; boxing gloves hanging on the ends of my arms soon reminded me! Why the hell did I let them do this to me? I needed a pee, which way was the bathroom? I was confused and began bumping into things. There was no carpet beneath my feet, I was walking on wood, how could that be? A dim light was switched on, it seemed I was in a wooden shed. Am I going crazy, how could I go to bed in five-star luxury and wake up in a hovel? I heard a key turning in the lock.

"Come on, Slave Boy, time to start work!" I recognised Jack's voice. A hand brushed my cheek but not in a caressing manner like last night. "How often do you shave?"

"What? I don't know, once a fortnight, I suppose. What's happening to me, Jack?"

"My partner and I are your masters and you will call us sir or master is that clear? No more first names, you understand?" His aggressive tone was for real.

"I don't want to play this game anymore, just give me my stuff and I'll find somewhere else!"

"I've obviously not made the situation very clear, you are our slave and you do as you're told. There is a list of chores for you to complete pinned on the back of the door. Do not try to escape, there are shutters on all doors and windows and the telephone is only accessible with a password. You will eat your meals in here."

"It's a pigsty, you can't expect me to live like this."

"The last boy survived for two years, if you clean it up you may last longer!"

"You can't be serious, he would have gone to the police when he got out!"

"He probably would have if he'd still been alive! In many ways he was a lot like you and of course nobody knew he was here."

I was beginning to believe he was speaking the truth especially when he said nobody knew I was here. "Why are you doing this to me, I thought we were friends."

"You are filling a vacancy. We need somebody to humiliate, to submit to our sexual desires and most importantly to obey."

"My classes begin next week . . ."

"I don't think you should concern yourself with further knowledge, you won't need it. This conversation is terminated, from now on you will get you're instructions in writing. Your bathroom is down the hall." He turned to leave but hesitated. "Failure to comply with your workload will result in painful punishment."

I snatched the printed page from the door and began reading; wash this, wash that, clean here, and there; the list was endless. It would take me a week to complete all these tasks. My first priority was the bathroom, I needed a pee real bad. To my horror the toilet was a hole in the floor and while emptying my bladder I searched for the second tap on the shower; I guessed right when I turned the water on—it was cold! With my teeth I managed to release the tightly wound chords on the boxing gloves and remove them. I stood under the shower, took a deep breath and turned on the water; it was freezing! The previous guy must have died of pneumonia! A rag of a towel was hardly big enough to dry my cock let alone the rest of my body.

I began the first job, scrubbing the kitchen floor! I made sure it was done thoroughly; I didn't want to do it a second time. Vacuuming the landing carpet was a doddle as was washing the paintwork on the stairs. The funny part was I began enjoying what I was doing. I stood back admiring my work . . .

A hood went over my head at the same time my arms were forced behind me and clamped together; I'd never been in handcuffs before but I guessed that's what they were. It was pointless trying to resist, there were two of them and both were stronger than me.

"You don't have to do this, I will submit to your demands you know that." Neither of them spoke as I was led down some stairs. I almost stumbled a couple times, being barefoot and unable to see while walking on uneven surfaces became a nightmare. A door opened and cool air hit my naked body, perhaps I was outside. I listened carefully for the sounds of birds or traffic but there was only silence. My wrist restraints were removed while I was laid on a narrow bench but ropes replaced the handcuffs pulling my arms above my head. The blackness was the worst part; not knowing if I was going to get my throat cut. Then I thought why go through all this trouble if I'm going to be killed?

"What do you want me to do?" I spoke through muffled cloth; still there was no reply.

Hands began roaming over my body and I felt the hood being loosened around my neck. It was lifted away from my mouth but not high enough for me to see, "come on guys I know who you are you don't have to play this game." I pleaded.

The head of a cock pressed against my lips; it wasn't Jack's or Mike's! In my brief experience of sucking cocks I could remember an aroma and this didn't smell of the heady perfumed shower gel they both used. This was more like Old Spice similar to my dad's aftershave. I was reluctant to open my mouth—that was until my balls were squeezed a little too tightly. The cock pushed rapidly into my throat causing me to choke, it withdrew enough for me to control the motion. The sides of my head were clamped between two hands that roughly forced my mouth to and fro on the monster cock. More hands touched, pressed and caressed my body triggering life into my dormant cock. It was obvious to me there were more than two people in the room; nobody had that many hands to thrill me!

Something wet was being spread on my lower stomach, around the base of my cock and over my balls. My cock was held firmly as an object glided gently over the prepared skin; they're shaving me! It took me eighteen years to grow the small amount of hair I had down there and now the bastards are mowing it away!

The guy straddling me began panting, his hands tried to crush my scull and then he came; a torrent of come hit the roof of my mouth and all I could do was swallow it.

Whispering in the background warned me of further torment and just as I predicted another cock was jammed into my mouth, they must be drawing straws to see who's next! I made myself as comfortable as possible while sucking on this shorter probe; this one had more foreskin and was easily satisfied as my tongue flicked across his helmet.

The mess around my middle was wiped dry with a cloth and a mouth immediately went down on my cock causing me to convulse with the unexpected pleasure. The guy I was sucking got a bonus too; I was passing my excitement onto him!

Somebody moved an apparatus and I recognised the metallic sound; I was in the gymnasium lying on a weightlifting bench! I remembered Jack telling me of a gymnasium in the basement of the house.

The guy above me squirted and my mind wasn't on the job, some of it was running down my cheek and it felt awful.

An unshaven face now smothered my cock, these strangers seemed to be taking it in turns. The spiky beard rubbed the inside of my thighs and did not feel good.

"I don't suppose there's any chance of a drink of water, Please don't think I'm complaining but this stuff is getting thick in my throat!" I said sarcastically.

Moments later my head was lifted and a vessel pressed against my lips; I drank the water until the glass was dry!

"Who is next or have I serviced you all!" I said boldly as the mouth on my cock changed yet again.

The slap across my face took me completely by surprise and my cock began to wilt. I can play that game as well; I thought of unpleasant things to make sure I received no satisfaction from the mouths and I was definitely not going to suck anyone else today! It had gone quiet, too quiet! What are they up to?

"If you're planning on killing me then think again, one or two people may be able to keep a secret but by the amount of cocks I've sucked I estimate there are at least twelve of you in the gymnasium. One of you will go to the police and you'll all end up in prison."

The hood was suddenly pulled from my head and my eyes squinted from the bright lights. Jack stood above me, "too late Slave Boy. They all left moments before your outburst which no doubt you realise you will be punished for!" He untied my bonds and pushed me up the stairs then led me back to my dungeon under the rear of the house.

I examined my shaved area and cursed myself for being naïve enough to accept help from a stranger on a train. Heaven knows what punishment those two fiends have got lined up for me.

I was getting hungry but first I needed a shower to get this stuff off me; it was over my face and in my hair, the bastards had wanked over my chest and stomach. Jesus I was in a mess!

The water seemed even colder than this morning and the bar of soap offered little assistance in removing the dried come. I persevered until I was satisfied all traces were washed away. Perhaps I should have left it stuck to my skin then the police could get DNA samples from my killers; too late now it's all down the drain! The towel was still wet from my shower earlier and I was cold; I lay on the makeshift bed curled up into a ball trying to get warm.

The key turned and the door opened, a tray of food and drink was placed on the floor, "can I have a blanket please, I'm cold."

"You should have thought about that before you opened your mouth, Slave Boy." Jack definitely had no compassion in his voice.

It was no real surprise that the meal consisted of dry bread and water. How could I maintain my strength on a diet like that?

I tried to sleep but bad dreams made sure I didn't get any rest. I had no idea of time, whether it was morning or evening or what day of the week it was. I may just as well have been on the moon.

"Slave Boy, wake up. It's time for your punishment." Jack's unmistakable voice again.

"What are you going to do to me?"

"You'll see when you get upstairs!"

Both were wearing their colourful Kimonos like they were having a party.

"You are going to watch a film with us." Mike stated.

I sat between them on the wide settee and was instructed to hold a cock in each hand and of course I obeyed. The film was of Jack and myself performing last night on the blue bed. Mike was beside himself with excitement as soon as it started, moaning with pleasure as I squeezed and pulled on his cock. Jack, on the other hand was more in control; then I remembered he had passed out before the session ended and was probably more interested to see how I responded. The film was at the point of entry and the camera didn't miss a thing; I could even see myself beating off.

Mike grabbed my hand, restricting further movement; he most likely wanted to save it until the end of the movie.

I watched Jack increase his rhythm, pumping my channel for all he was worth, then all motion stopped except for me.

The master to my right allowed me to continue the hand action as I squirmed on screen all over the bed trying to catch the jets of come flying in all directions. My hand was drenched in Mike's fluid but the other hand was dry as Jack watched the TV showing my concerned face, thinking he was dead.

Mike used a towel to remove the mess he'd made while I sat on the settee with a handful of cum. "Wipe it clean on yourself and don't let it drip on the carpet!" He instructed. The stuff appeared to be turning into water and I quickly spread it over my stomach and thighs remembering how it sets like glue after a while.

Jack finished his brandy, placed his glass on the coffee table and stood up; his semi erection poking through the gap in his short gown. "Stand up Slave Boy, let me examine my colleague's handiwork!"

My master was on his knees studying closely the shaved area; he pulled my cock one way then the other, lifted it up to scrutinize the sack and finally felt around my hole. "Go get the equipment, there's more!" He told master number two.

The wide glass-topped coffee table was cleared and I was spread eagled on it face down with my legs pulled wide apart, cool liquid was sprayed around my hole but I felt no razor this time and after a few minutes the wetness was wiped away. I guessed it was something women used on their legs and fanny's. Neither Jack nor Mike said a word to each other which suggested to me this wasn't the first time they had carried out this de-furring operation.

"Stand up!" Jack startled me. "Your punishment will begin shortly!"

"But I thought that was my punishment!" I protested.

"We have to teach you a lesson for speaking out of turn in front of my guests this afternoon." Jack continued.

A chair was carefully positioned in the centre of the room, my guess being it was there for the cameras to focus on. Mike took off his Kimono and sat on the aforementioned chair then beckoned me to him. I had a sudden dread of what was going to happen and I was right.

"Lay over his legs, you are going to be spanked!" Jack commanded but I hesitated. "If you don't I'll get out the whip then you'll really know what pain is!" Although unwilling to comply I knew the alternative could leave me scarred for life.

Mike didn't even try to conceal his erection as I crawled over his open thighs, his damp cock head pressing into what used to be my pubic region and had I been bigger than a dwarf my hands and feet may have reached the floor but as it was I dangled and swayed waiting for the first slap.

From the corner of my eye I witnessed Jack operate the remote to start the cameras rolling and I was tempted to shout 'action, take one' but thought better of it—the idea of being whipped scared the shit out of me.

Slap! Mike's massive hand hit my bum cheek so hard it almost knocked me off the chair and it hurt like hell, "Jesus Christ, go easy!" I complained.

"We can always go straight for the whip, Slave Boy, if you prefer!" Jack was a bastard!

The second slap was delayed until I shook my head. Whack! My head lifted up and I bit my lip to prevent me from crying out. The third was just as fierce but I seemed to be getting used to it and began counting the seconds between spanks; thirty seconds passed before the next punishing blow struck my sore cheeks but between each one Mike's hand was caressing the glowing area and I could feel his hardness pulsating against my own cock which was beginning to expand by itself. I had counted eight violent whacks so far and had no idea how many more there were to come but my mind was on other things, namely my responding cock! How could I get excited through pain?

My cock head was nudging against Mike's and he must have felt it . . .

"Ten, that's enough for now, we'll see if you have learned anything by this time tomorrow. Go back to your kennel, Slave Boy, food and water will be brought to you later and take a shower you look awful!

I clamped my hands over my erection, ran from the lounge, along the corridor and down into my cell. The dim light cast eerie shadows as I made my way over rough wood to the shower. The first thing I noticed was a proper towel; just an insignificant thing like that made me feel a lot better and that wasn't all, the tiny piece of soap had been replaced with a bottle of the sweet smelling gel but most importantly there was a toothbrush and toothpaste! Unfortunately the water was still as cold as ice but I had to persevere and clean my body of Mike's spent spunk! I was drying when I heard the key turn.

"Food is on the floor don't knock it over!" His Master's Voice came to mind! "And if you touch yourself in the night it'll be the boxing gloves again!"

The tray of food looked different; apart from the bread and water there was a bowl of what smelled like soup and it tasted wonderful, I must be pleasing my masters. A thin mattress, probably from a cheap sun-bed along with a smelly blanket was on the floor where I slept last night and I hastily wrapped myself in the itchy material; my body was still cold after the shower!

I was having one horrible dream after another, why can't I go off to sleep?

Someone was unlocking the door, I recognised the smell of Mike, my nose had become very sensitive to odours since the afternoon session in the gym.

"You want me, Master?" I asked politely for fear of getting further punishment.

"Suck my cock like you did before and be quick!" He demanded.

I bet he's sneaked down here without Jack knowing. I swallowed his long, thick cock and gave him as much of a thrill as I could. My own cock was solid but I remembered Jack's threat earlier. I was used to jerking off several times a day and this restriction was taking some getting used to.

My tongue seemed to be my salvation; all the time I could give satisfaction I would be in good favour with my masters. I sucked and licked, touched and squeezed until I sensed the incoming tide and then it was over. A maximum of five minutes but it could earn me another bowl of soup tomorrow. Mike's last words before he left were, "I wasn't down here tonight, remember that!"

The blanket provided warmth and the thin, scrawny mattress a degree of comfort and eventually I slept.

Chapter 3

I WAS SITTING AT the end of my bed when the door was unlocked. Jack placed the food on the floor and pinned at list of chores for me to complete.

"Thank you, Master!" I said respectfully; he didn't respond.

Today's list included the gymnasium where I knew there would be clotted come from yesterday; not all of it fell onto me. I ate my bread and drank the water while studying the routine. A quick cold shower revived me and after cleaning my teeth I felt like a new man, any man in fact, I had a hard-on like never before. It had been a couple of days since relieving myself but I knew I was being watched and the threat of the whip was enough to deter me from doing it to myself.

I washed the apparatus in the gymnasium until it shined, I could see my reflection in the floor as well as the mirrors. I would have eaten a meal from the toilet floor after I had scrubbed it spotless. I was positive that area was the cleanest it had ever been; I just hoped my masters would see it that way! The next on the list was the dining table, it had to be French polished! Instructions had been copied from a 'How to . . ." on the computer and all the materials were in a bucket by the table. This was going to be a challenge . . .

"You fuck this table up and you will get a thousand lashes, understand Slave Boy?" Jack was in a foul mood.

"Yes Master, I'll follow the instructions to the letter."

"Mike has gone to work in the city so you will prepare a meal for me at one o'clock."

"Yes Master, what would you like?"

"Surprise me!"

As I unpacked the stuff from the bucket I let my imagination run wild as to what I would dish up for my Master but it wouldn't be coq-au-vin. The work on the table was progressing well as lunchtime approached. I peeled potatoes and carrots in the shape of phallic symbols, fried some chicken and made some special sauce out of something I was forbidden to do! At precisely one o'clock I walked into the dining room with the meal and placed it in front of my Master.

"Pour me a glass of wine, Slave Boy." He said sternly. I obeyed, bowed and left the room with a contented smile on my face.

I spent the rest of the afternoon polishing the table. Mike returned home at six and immediately demanded brandy. He stripped out of his clothes and as I handed him the glass our eyes made contact and his cock went horizontal. I ran to the dining room and continued work on the table.

"Where's Jack?" Mike asked quietly.

"I think he went to bed, he looked tired." I continued rubbing the linseed oil on the table. Mike moved closer behind me his erection at forty-five degrees; it nudged between my cheeks as I leaned over the wide table.

"Let's not cause World War Three!" I suggested.

"How dare you speak to me like that, you are getting above your station Slave Boy. You are only here to satisfy my needs, how I want and when I want." He jammed his cock head between my cheeks.

"If you are going to fuck me then at least wear a rubber, it could be for your own protection as well." I never stopped working while the exchange took place.

"You little shit, you're going to regret ever walking into this house!"

"Don't you think I've done that already? Look, I'll play your little game until you get fed up with me and find some other idiot. I'll suck your cock, give you a wank, or whatever, but you are not ever going to put your cock up my arse unless you wear a condom, is that clear?"

The slap across my face almost knocked me off my feet, he may well have been in his forty's but he still had a lot of strength.

"Get to your den and don't expect any food tonight!"

I gathered up all the stuff, returned it to the bucket then went back to my dump and sulked; my big mouth got me into trouble! I must learn to think before I speak. The cold water in the shower was no comfort for the traumatic event. I stood under the spray for as long as I could washing the oil and shellac from my skin. I dried and sat on the mattress trying to think of how I might get myself out of this mess. Escape, it seemed, was not an option; the telephone needed a password but what about a computer? There must be one somewhere; I could send a message to my parents . . . But I didn't know where I was, it was almost dark when I'd arrived here. All I knew is that I got off a train and ended up in a tree lined avenue . . .

"Get up, Slave Boy, I hear you've been naughty again." Jack was awake!

Mike stood in the centre of the lounge; he was naked, semi-erect and held a short handled whip in his hand. It looked like a medieval cat-o-nine tails I'd read about in history books.

"No way! You're not using that on me! Just because I wouldn't let you shove your cock up me without protection, that's unfair!"

Mike beckoned me to him but I stood my ground. A hand gripped the back of my neck and forced me towards the instrument of severe pain. I fell to the ground at Mike's feet.

"I have done nothing wrong," I said staring at the floor, "I have carried out my duties, submitted to your demands and never complained about being your slave. How can you justify punishing me for asking for protected sex. You know as well as I do the dangers of catching the unmentionable disease. If I'm guilty of speaking my mind then punish me, if not then let me go back to my shed."

Jack began clapping, "Nice speech, Slave Boy, but you seem to have forgotten something; it doesn't matter to us whether you catch anything or not. You've already told us you were a virgin when you arrived here so we're not likely to catch anything from you, are we? Let the punishment commence!"

I was laid across the glass-topped coffee table like before and gripped the sides in anticipation of pain. My bum cheeks still ached from the slaps of last night but I mustn't let them see I'm afraid.

Something strange touched my bum, it was damp and tender; one cheek then the other was caressed with the sensation, was this a prelude to severe pain, an anaesthetic or was something sinister about to happen to me.

"You can get up now, you've passed the submissive test!" Jack's voice had mellowed.

I slowly relaxed my grip and waited for Mike to countermand my reprieve, it was the sick sort of thing they would do.

Hands on either side of my body assisted me to stand up. Two smiling faces looked into my eyes and I began to cry.

Arms surrounded my shaking body offering comfort to my traumatised mind. I sat on the settee and was offered a large brandy.

When I had calmed down and realised this was not another trick, Jack explained the reason for tormenting me in such a ghastly manner.

"You wanted to know about the gay scene and what it could be like, you have gained a lifetime experience in just a few days. It may have been harsh at times, even painful, but you have found out a few things about yourself that could have taken years. You're a good cook, enjoy pain, love discipline, never afraid of work but not once did you try to play Mike against me even when you knew it would cause trouble, that says a lot about a person. Now you can make the choice yourself; do you want to be master or slave?"

"I don't know; I've not tried being master yet!"

Chapter 4

YEARS PASSED, I FINISHED with honours at Vale and became a lawyer joining a major firm dealing in accident claims.

"Here's your list for today, Martin." My pretty secretary fluttered her eyelashes at me as she had every day since I joined the firm. If only she knew!

My first client that day was a nineteen-year-old motorcyclist who had been knocked from his machine by a drunken motorist. As soon as he walked, or rather limped, into my office I saw the most beautiful young man I'd ever seen in my life. His blue eyes, high cheek bones, unblemished skin and the most gorgeous smile ever, sent an instant message to my cock and he was still fully dressed! We shook hands and I held onto his longer than was necessary.

"Good morning, John, I'm Martin and will be dealing with your case. I've read the report and think the firm have an excellent chance of getting a sizeable amount of compensation for you."

"How long will it take?"

"Well, this claim, like all the others, will be contested by the insurance company so it could take up to a year."

He began to sob. "What am I supposed to do until then, I've got no money, I've lost my job because of the accident, and my landlord is throwing me out at the weekend for not paying my rent."

"Now, now, don't upset yourself." I reached across the desk and gripped his trembling hands in mine. "I'm sure something will turn up. Have you no family or friends who could support you until your settlement comes though?"

His hands held mine tightly, his tearful, pleading eyes begging for a way out of his misery, "there's nobody; my family threw me out when they found out I was gay. Can't you help me, Martin, I'll do anything you ask?"

"Well," I began slowly and looking deep into those beautiful tearful eyes, "I could do with some help; you see, I've just purchased an old building, miles out of town. It used to belong to a plantation owner many years ago . . .

The End

THE RECRUIT

Chapter 1

"YES, WHAT DO YOU want?" Sergeant Brown asked abruptly as the timid youth stood at the guardhouse door.

"I've been told to report here."

"Sergeant! You see these three stripes? You call me sergeant when you speak to me, you horrible little man!"

"Yes sergeant, sorry sergeant!" The teenager repeated. The non-commissioned officer was right in one respect; the boy was small, barely five-feet-seven inches tall.

"Wait over there while I find out what to do with you," he took the brown envelope from the outstretched hand then picked up his schedule and studied it for a moment, "according to my list there are no recruits arriving until Friday, that's three days from now." He began dialling and then, as the voice on the other end answered, stood to attention.

Captain Barry took the call, "What do you mean a new recruit? The next intake isn't until Friday. OK sergeant, send him to me, I'll find him something to do until the new batch arrives." He replaced the receiver and continued looking through his binoculars at the young soldiers on the assault course. "Now that one I wouldn't kick out of bed for a week . . ." he muttered quietly to himself.

A knock on the door caused the captain to sit at his desk concealing his erection before calling loudly, "enter!"

The new boy stood in the doorway not knowing what to do. "Well don't just stand there letting in the cold air, shut the dammed door. Sit there while I go through your papers." Captain Barry loved boys between the ages of eighteen to twenty-five and when he saw the Adonis sitting before him he had great difficulty in reading the documents given him. "So, you are John Smith, nineteen-years-old and come from Newark, is that correct?"

"Yes, Sir!"

"Right, the first thing to do is get you kitted out the second is have a haircut." He pressed a bell on his desk and his clerk, Corporal Jones, marched in and saluted, "take recruit Smith to the quartermasters then to the barbers and back to me." The officer stood up to his full height of six feet and two inches.

"Yes sir!"

Captain Barry resumed his position at the window, his lower body pressed against the warm radiator while he studied the young soldiers being yelled at by the physical training instructor. The punishment should soon be over for them and they will be taking a shower in the room next door, "I don't want any interruptions for the next half hour", he hummed quietly to himself as he moved a picture of the queen slightly to look through the spy hole. The exhausted mud-covered squad began stripping out of their T-shirts and shorts, the showers were turned on and there they were, naked cherubs soaping themselves; so many beautiful cocks all in one room!

Every day at the same time, Captain Barry would take out his enormous cock and beat off while watching his troops clean themselves, the same troops that he would scream and shout at on morning parade, only today would be different!

John Smith, now dressed in khaki, gazed at himself in the barber's mirror and thought he was looking at someone else. Most of his long blond hair was lying on the floor; his sad eyes made contact with the sheerer who just shrugged his shoulders and began work on his next victim.

Corporal Jones looked up from his newspaper, "come on, Smith, I'll take you back to Captain Barry." They marched towards to the block of offices, it was early March and a cool wind blew across the parade ground but once inside the main door it felt warm. The phone rang and Corporal Jones raced to answer it before anyone else, he indicated for Smith to go into Captain Barry's office so he could take the call in private.

John Smith was very naive and unaccustomed to knocking before entering, hence when he saw Captain Barry with his trousers around his ankles, staring closely at a picture of the queen and furiously beating off he was a little bemused! He waited silently until the captain moaned, arched his back and shot streams of cum up the partition.

The officer wiped his drooling cock on his underwear, pulled up his trousers and was about realign the picture when he saw the new recruit standing by the closed door.

"What are you doing in here?" He screamed loud enough to rattle the windows.

"You told me to report back after I had my haircut, sir."

"What did you see when you entered my office?"

John Smith may have been naïve but he wasn't stupid. "I saw you adjusting the picture of the queen, sir."

"And that is exactly what I was doing. If I hear you have been spreading gossip you will spend the rest of your army career in the glass-house."

John sat by himself in the cookhouse, everyone else had been in the army longer than him and had made friends already so after his evening meal he marched back to his dormitory—a long hut with twelve beds, six on each side with an ablution room at the far end—the small building had been closed up for a week and it felt warm and cosy. He took a shower then climbed into bed and began reading the book he'd bought at Newark railway station.

Captain Barry was furious with himself for not locking the door but even more outraged with the new recruit catching him with his pants down. He sat on his bed in the officer's quarters mulling over what to do, then an idea came to mind to teach the lad a lesson.

The book was good but his eyes ached, the fluorescent tube was flashing at the far end of the room and John found it distracting. He switched off the light and snuggled under the covers.

Captain Barry removed his uniform and donned his black tight fitting tracksuit along with a navy blue ski mask his mother had knitted him. He opened the door to his room and making sure nobody was around crept out of a side exit and into the wooded area between the officers mess and the lowly other ranks. He knew exactly where John fucking Smith would be on his first night in barracks.

A sudden noise woke John, and for a moment he had to remember where he was, he turned and laid on his back with his fingers locked together behind his head looking up into the blackness.

A hand went over his mouth and a threatening voice whispered. "One sound and I'll slit your throat!" The mask hid the real sound of the captain and John was terrified, too scared even to remove his hands from behind his head. The disguised officer pulled the covers from the bed and began feeling for the body lying on it. John was naked, he'd slept that way for years and never gave it a second thought that there could be others who may not find it acceptable. A hand was on the lower part of his leg and moving slowly upwards towards his knee. He was petrified; his mouth had gone dry and worst of all he could feel movement in his cock. He was vulnerable lying there with no clothes.

But Captain Barry was in for the surprise of his life as his hand moved further up the inside of boy's right thigh, he felt goose bumps on the smooth skin, then the hairless ball sack came into contact with the searching fingers. A sigh escaped from the officer's lips and as his hand crept higher it touched the base of John's swollen cock. The officer's hands were big, he'd taken part in most sports since he was young, was a keen boxer and enjoyed weight training and when he had difficulty grasping John's wide cock he couldn't believe his luck and that wasn't all; as he reached for the young soldiers crown it was about nine inches further away lying on his stomach like an iron bar!

John lay frozen to the bed, too frightened to move or call out. A smooth hand was sliding very gently up and down his ever-so rigid cock. He was ashamed that he couldn't control what was happening to him; the only person ever to touch his cock was himself. He was petrified of moving in case the aggressor went through with his threat so he remained still and allowed the mystery hand to continue with the caressing motion.

Captain Barry wanted that cock in his mouth more than anything he'd desired in his life, he pictured in his mind the boy's long blond locks before they were chopped off by the Barber of Seville. That same beautiful boy with an enormous cock was lying in front of him just waiting to be deflowered. The officer pulled off the ski mask and moved his face closer to the fat, warm steel rod. The scent of freshly washed cock hit his nostrils, the smell of perfumed soap hung like a halo over the gorgeous flesh, it took him to cloud nine and he hadn't even tasted it yet! The captain lifted the straining column from the youth's stomach and with tongue out began licking the underside of John's crown.

The nineteen-year-old moaned loudly with delight as the wetness skimmed over the sensitive gland, his hands moved down from behind his head and blindly grabbed the ears of the mysterious intruder who had threatened him with death just five minutes earlier. John felt hot lips cover the whole of his helmet and began quivering as the mouth slowly moved down to the base of his cock. He gripped the ears firmly fearing he would cum if the movement continued upwards.

Meanwhile the captain didn't give a damn whether he pleased the boy or not, he was only interested in his own desire and pulled the clinging hands off his ears. Up and down, up and down, his head setting up a rhythm but the body beneath him began fidgeting.

"I'm coming, oh Jesus Christ, I'm coming!" John shouted rather too loudly for the Captain's liking; he swiftly placed a hand over the recruit's mouth.

Captain Barry gagged at so much fluid being pumped down his throat, never in his life had he swallowed that much nectar in one session. He removed his face from the weakening pole, disappointed it hadn't lasted longer. Perhaps he could think of another situation and do it again.

If it wasn't for the door closing John would never had known the visitor had gone. He had been afraid for his life at first but had enjoyed every minute of the wonderful sensation. "Can we do it again tomorrow?" He called. But it fell onto deaf ears; the man in black was back in his room already. He removed his tracksuit and stepped into the shower, he was hot and sticky and needed to wash his mouth of boy-cum.

Chapter 2

JOHN LAY ON HIS bed mesmerised by the incident, his cock regained its strength as he reminisced in his mind the events of the last half hour. This time his hand took over where the lips had been racing up and down and the same thing happened; only the mess ended up over his stomach and chest instead of inside the other guy's mouth. He took a shower, picked up the bedcovers and went back to the land of dreams.

Not so for the captain; he had a problem sleeping, something was keeping him awake but for the life of him he couldn't think what it might be. He tossed and turned, even jerked off to the memory of the blond recruit and still had trouble dropping off. The alarm clock woke him at six, he felt lousy at the lack of proper rest. "It's going to be fucking freezing on the parade ground this morning!" He said to himself as he looked at the white grass from his window. He hung last night's tracksuit in the wardrobe and closed a drawer—the drawer; that's what had kept him awake for most of the night, he had taken the ski mask from the drawer but it wasn't there now! "Oh no! I left it in Smith's bed." He slapped his face with both hands; furious with himself for being so stupid.

As John climbed out of bed his feet were tangled in some woolly material; he picked it up and studied the dark blue cloth, a smile crept across his face as he thought of what it might be handy for—catching the cum at night so it doesn't mess up the sheets!

"Thank you, sergeant. You can dismiss the men!" Captain Barry was glad the parade finished early, he hated the cold and to make things worse it began to rain. He marched at a rapid pace back to his office, saluting every few steps at smart young recruits trying their best to impress him. He was a little taken aback at the sight of Smith waiting outside his office. "What do *you* want?"

"Corporal Jones said you needed someone to clean your office, sir." John looked the officer straight in the eye.

"Yes, I do. The lad that normally does the cleaning is on leave. Follow me." He unlocked the door to his office and both entered. "You'll find everything you need in that cupboard. You'll clean the tops of those beams as well, they haven't been touched for years, expect to get dirty. Get on with it!"

John dragged a tall set of steps under the first of the roof beams and with a bucket of soapy water and wet cloth began the boring task of wood-washing. Captain Barry left the office with a pile of papers saying he would be back when the work was finished. In reality, he didn't want his uniform covered in dust!

The officer's first stop was last night's room of passion; only it wasn't lust he was after it was the ski mask! He searched the bed, the floor, John's locker. "Where the fuck is it?" He raged to himself.

The youth completed his chores and sat waiting for his boss to return. The clock on the wall didn't seem to move and he was becoming fidgety; there were photos of previous 'passing out parades' pasted around the walls and bored John began scrutinising them in the unlikely event he saw someone he knew. The portrait of the queen hung at eye level, 'that's where the captain was playing with himself yesterday', John remembered. The tiniest of holes had been drilled through to the next room and when the recruit pressed his eye against it he was amazed at just how much he could see into the changing room. Suddenly, John heard the captain talking to his clerk and busied himself with a duster to make out he had been working all day.

"Haven't you finished yet, Smith?"

"Yes sir, it's all done."

"Just look at the state of you! You can't march back to your barrack room like that. Go next door, take a shower and brush your uniform clean. You'll find some towels in the locker."

When John entered the changing room he noted where the hole was and made sure he was directly in line with it. He slowly removed his clothes, shaking the dust out of each garment and folding it neatly on the bench then dropped his underwear while his back was towards the peephole. He flexed his muscles for a few moments before running his fingers though his very short hair then stepped into the shower. With the soap he spread the foamy cream over his skin paying particular attention to his cock and balls; he rubbed himself until he became hard then rubbed some more; in fact he just kept cleaning his cock and balls until they shone! He sent jets of cum up the shower wall then washed the evidence away. He towelled himself dry, dressed back in his uniform and returned to the office remembering to knock on the door first.

"Enter!" Came the reply.

"Thank you for letting me take a shower sir, I feel a lot cleaner now!" John collected the cleaning materials and stowed them in the cupboard close to the queen's portrait, "shall I clean this mess up sir, it looks like somebody has spilt something on the floor." he knew exactly what it was but wasn't expecting the reply.

Captain Barry was a canny officer and wasn't going to be hoodwinked by some raw recruit. "I can't imagine what that might be, why don't you dip your finger in it and taste it!"

"I'd rather not do that, sir."

"It wasn't a request, Smith!" He bellowed.

John reluctantly touched the liquid with his middle finger and was about to lick it.

"Now how can you possibly hope to find out what it tastes like with a tiny drop like that? Scoop it up and drink it!" He shouted loudly.

John shuddered as his cupped hands got closer to his mouth, if he smelled it first he would probably throw up so it would have to be quick. He tilted his head back and allowed the fast flowing liquid to fall into his throat then wiped his mouth with the back of his hand. "I didn't recognise the taste, sir. It was nothing that has passed my lips before."

The captain looked closely into Smiths eyes, "don't ever think you can get one over on me. I've been in this army a lot longer than you!"

John stood to attention, "yes, sir, shall I report here tomorrow?"

"Yes, nine o'clock sharp!"

The clerk, Corporal Jones, looked up as he left the office. "What did you do to make him so mad? He could be heard miles away."

"I caught him making love to the queen!" The corporal's mouth dropped low enough to see his tonsils while his eyeballs looked as if they would drop from their sockets!

For a second evening John ate his meal alone in the cookhouse while other boys laughed and made a lot of noise around him. He accepted his loneliness thinking he would soon make friends with the new intake on Friday. Back in his quiet room he tried reading but the flickering light bothered him. He pulled a bed to the centre of the room, balanced a chair on it then climbed up and with some difficulty managed to twist and loosen the offending tube; it stayed off. He stripped out of his clothes, climbed into bed and began reading again.

Captain Barry was also lying on his bed but wasn't reading; he was scheming! After watching Smith in the shower he was determined to have another feel of the beautiful soft skin. He needed a disguise to cover his face; the last thing he needed was to be recognised by anyone while visiting the other ranks quarters. He searched his wardrobe until he found the keffiyeh he wore a couple of years ago while on manoeuvres in Bahrain. He folded the dark material then, viewing his image in the mirror, wound it around his head, "Lawrence of Arabia, eat your heart out, tonight the pretty boy is mine!" He spoke softly to himself then donned the black tracksuit, pulled on his trainers and sneaked out the side door as before.

The small barrack block was in darkness; he turned the handle of the door and crept to John's bed. He listened to the shallow breathing then slowly lifted the covers and as luck would have it the cloudless sky allowed the moon to highlight the naked form lying on his back with his hands behind his head like last night. John's cock was sleeping, resting on his right thigh, even in its dormant state it was a wonderful sight. The officer was obsessed with the cock more than its owner and leaning over the tired youth he began smelling the aroma, his nose just a millimetre from the skin; then his tongue gently ran the length from base to tip then back again. The sleeping giant was awakening, blood was pumping into the flesh and it was growing by the second. John moaned quietly as if in a dream unaware that his cock was moving from the nine o'clock position to twelve! Captain Barry had found a new toy and he wasn't going to lose it; he held the base in his hand, lifting the head towards his mouth but the damned keffiyeh got in the way. He yanked the material away from his face and had another attempt at swallowing the scrumptious cock.

A sudden crash of breaking glass caused John to sit up fast like he'd been given an electric shock. His head came into contact with an object of about the same size and it sounded like two cocoanuts being knocked together, "Ouch! Jesus Christ!" He shouted.

Captain Barry saw stars and thought he'd been hit in the face with a cricket bat; he bit his lower lip to stop himself from crying out with the pain then ran from the room slamming the door behind him.

John felt the dampness on his erection as he climbed out of bed; he switched on the light and was annoyed at himself for sleeping while the mysterious stranger had taken advantage of him. On surveying the dormitory he could see the remains of the shattered fluorescent tube he had fiddled with earlier. He needed a pee but as he tried to move his feet they became entangled in a large square of black material. John laughed to himself. "He's leaving me clues to who he is!"

The frustrated officer looked at his bruised cheek in the bathroom mirror, "I'm going to have a fucking black eye by the morning! That little bastard is going to pay dearly for this!" He said out loud then looked for his keffiyeh! "I don't fucking believe it, I've done it again, shit and shit again!"

Chapter 3

"WHAT HAPPENED TO YOUR face, Smith?" Corporal Jones asked John as he waited outside the officer's door.

"I think I bumped into something during the night, I can't remember doing it."

"Stand up!" Jones shouted as Captain Barry strolled at a fast pace into the outer office. "Morning sir!" Standing to attention he saluted and watched as the officer shot into his room and closed the door. "Was he wearing sunglasses?" The clerk asked in surprise.

John knocked on the door and entered, the officer tried to hide his face from the recruit by putting his hand against his forehead. "Have you something for me to do, sir?"

What Captain Barry wanted to say was 'bring back my ski mask and keffiyeh, you little bastard' but instead ordered him to clean up the changing room and showers. With Smith occupied the captain searched the recruit's room again for his missing items, finally coming to the conclusion they had been thrown away. "How dare the little bastard discard my ski mask, it was a present from my mother." He muttered under his breath as he left the room.

John began the arduous job of scrubbing the wooden benches and shower trays. It was hot, the radiators had been set high so that the soldiers returning from the gruelling assault course would have a warm place to strip out of their wet and muddy gear. The sweat began running down the inside of his uniform, he couldn't work like this! He removed his clothes down to his underwear and continued mopping the floor.

As it approached four o'clock he gathered his cleaning stuff and placed it by the door then grabbed a towel and stood under the shower but just as he was about to turn on the water about twenty cold and sodden lads ran in and began undressing. Some were laughing, others complaining but it was obvious all were glad to be inside and warm. John was mesmerised by the naked bodies and wondered if it was one of them visiting him at night. He studied each one individually, their faces, bodies and especially their cocks.

"Look at him!" One of the boys pointed at John, "he's got a hard on!"

As if he was giving away chocolate bars they all ran into his cubicle and began laughing and giggling, pressing their bodies against his and touching, they all wanted to feel the enormous steel rod pointing towards the ceiling. Several had erections as they played around and teased each other but John just stood against the wall filled with embarrassment! He didn't mind being watched through the hole in the wall as long as he didn't have to scoop up the juice again!

Captain Barry had never witnessed anything quite like it; he came three times while watching the antics of the recruits as they frolicked together with John. Oh, how he wished he could be with them! But they were playing with *his* toy, how dare they touch the beautiful flesh he had become obsessed with?

"I've cleaned the shower and changing room, sir. Is there anything else you would like me to do?" The officer would love to have told John to take off his clothes and lay over the desk ready to be fucked but instead told him to report back at nine tomorrow morning.

The evening meal was a delight for John; a couple of recruits from the shower recognised him and sat at his table. The three of them chatted long after most had left the cookhouse and when the duty sergeant told them to leave they ended up at John's hut. Pete, a dark-haired boy of eighteen years spoke of a strange experience the night he arrived, Ray interrupted, "did someone sit on your bed and play with your cock?"

"Yes, why, did somebody do it to you as well?" Pete asked in surprise.

"It's happened to me the past two nights; I'm half expecting him back tonight," John told them, "the funny thing is, he leaves me a clue like he wants me to know who he is; the first night it was a ski mask and the second this piece of black material."

"What time does he get here?" Pete asked.

"It was about ten o'clock the first night but I was asleep the second time, why?"

"How about if we hide in the shadows and wait for him." Ray was thinking along the same lines as his friend.

"Ok, but do nothing until he's finished, I quite enjoy it!" All three burst out laughing.

Captain Barry was contemplating whether to chance his luck again, he was almost caught out last night and had the bruise to prove it. But every time he shut his eyes all he could see were muddy hands smothering that magnificent cock; he must have one last try! Dark tracksuit and trainers were worn but he had nothing to cover his face, "I'll chance it tonight, it'll be the last time, the new intake will be here tomorrow," he muttered to himself as he opened his door.

"Bit late to be going jogging, old fellow!" Captain Jenkins stepped from the bathroom just as Captain Barry entered the corridor. "My word, what have you done to your eye."

"I slipped in the bath," he lied. What he really wanted to say was 'mind your own fucking business, you lily-white pussy'.

He knew the way to the barrack room like the back of his hand; he had trodden the ground hundreds of times since his posting last year. Every intake had its special recruit, the one that stood out from all the rest and he had taken advantage of his officer status to examine each and every one of them usually through the hole but on the odd occasion in their huts late at night, like tonight. He glanced at the luminous dial of his imitation Rolex; it was a little after ten and all lights were out in Smith's room.

As the handle turned, Pete and Ray tiptoed to the ablutions at the rear of the hut while John lay on his back with fingers locked behind his head as usual, feigning sleep. The bed covers were slowly removed and dropped to the floor, the room was warm, much warmer than before and Captain Barry was perspiring already. He pulled the tracksuit top over his head, then began removing the trousers but the trainers were in the way. He used his left foot to ease off the right shoe and vice-versa; now completely naked he sat on the edge of the bed and began stroking John's slack flesh. Within seconds the boy's third arm began to swell, rising gradually passed his belly button; the moon was full and it beamed through the window for a second night placing his quarry in the spotlight; the splendid cock just waiting to be sucked.

The officer carefully prised the stiffness from the youth's stomach then his mouth went down covering the crown with his soft, wet lips. John moaned with pleasure but didn't move, this was by far the most thrilling thing that had happened to him in his short life! The slurping continued, slowly at first but gathering speed all the time. The recruit wanted it to last all night but at this rate it would all be over in seconds. He moved his head from side to side like he was dreaming then unhurriedly brought his arms down by his sides resting his right hand on the officer's thigh. John's fingers reached out and felt the stiffness in his grasp; his thumb located the slippery juice and stirred it around Captain Barry's helmet causing him to tremble with the unexpected pleasure.

The two recruits in hiding could see clearly what was going on; Ray began undressing, he too was feeling the heat. Pete followed suit and both moved closer to the action.

John Smith's mystery man was in a world of his own, not only did he have the most mouth-watering cock between his lips but also the softest hands ever were stroking his meat. But when something touched his shoulder he almost had a heart attack! He freed his tight lipped grip from Smith's cock, swiftly turned his head and came face to face with another hard piece of flesh. He overcame his fright by sucking hard on the new erection gaining further excitement listening to the boy's sighs! Yet another cock was placed in his hand; this one was circumcised like the recruit he had a couple of weeks ago. Could it be the same one?

John sat up watching the performance, his thriller, now kneeling on the bed, had the body of an athlete; his strong arms hung from wide shoulders, the powerful chest heaved and fell, he had tight stomach muscles and a slender waist, and all were supported on sturdy thighs. Unfortunately his face was in the shadows but his cock wasn't! The fat, iron hard pole was pointing at his face; there's a first time for everything, he thought, 'if I don't like it I don't have to do it again' and without a second to waste leaned forward and took it in his mouth.

In all the ten years Captain Barry had spent serving queen and country he had never known an evening like this; he had a cock in his mouth, one in his hand and a beautiful blond boy sucking on his pole. His hips gyrated forcing himself deeper into Smith's throat; he wanted to scream out with joy but knew he would be recognised.

Pete, on the right side of the bed, held onto the officer's swinging balls as they swayed to and fro like a pendulum, his other hand explored the firm buttocks, groping the warm passage and poking a finger into the moist hole. It was almost too much for the captain; his hands snatched at Smith's head stopping all movement for a few seconds until the juice drained back down the tube!

The light from the moon had faded, only blackness prevailed but it didn't slow down the action, if anything it increased. Positions changed and it was the officer who was lying on the bed with Smith straddling his chest, lunging nine inches of hard warm steel into his throat while the two other youths were taking it in turns to smother his cock with their mouths. A hand moved slowly up to his chest into short downy hair and touched his nipple; he heaved and sighed a little too loudly. Fingers pinched at the spiky point forcing him to squirm with ecstasy.

John arched his back as he felt the warm spray splash his skin probably from one of the boys behind him; another torrent of tepid liquid joined the first. It was too much for the new recruit and without warning emptied his cock down the captain's throat;

All three youths now concentrated their energy on the mystery-man's fat meat, six hands touched, felt and squeezed; different pairs of lips pleasured his helmet and balls, more fingers delved into the opening and then a hand wrapped itself around the base of the stem slowly working the loose skin up and down. John felt the eruption building inside his fist and lunged forward with his mouth covering the bulbous head just in time to catch the lava spraying from inside the crater. Although warm, it tasted vaguely like the cold stuff Captain Barry made him drink in his office!

Four exhausted bodies flopped over each other on the narrow bed; it was John who asked the obvious question. "Who are you?"

One of Captain Barry's talents was acting, from an early age he had wanted to be on the stage and had a lucky break while still at school. A production of a Gilbert and Sullivan opera was witnessed by the owner of an acting academy for young people and he was thrilled to be invited to take free lessons. He learned a lot while attending the weekly classes and became proficient in copying accents. Tonight this gift was going to get him out of trouble.

"I am the Man in Black," his Scottish delivery would have fooled anyone from Glasgow, "I can't reveal my identity; it could get us all into trouble. Now I must leave, you'll not be seeing me again." He climbed over the tangled limbs and began dressing.

"But you left me things, a ski mask and a black scarf, were they presents?" John asked.

"Where are these items now, I should take them with me."

"You'll get them when we do it again."

"I will be in touch soon, do not put the light on and don't follow me!"

That would be unlikely, John thought, we're not dressed.

The three recruits sat on John's bed mulling over the night's events, "maybe it's the barber," Ray considered.

"I think the barber's Welsh," Pete reckoned.

"Well, whoever he is, we'll have to wait to find out. Help me turn this mattress over there's not a dry spot on it!" John laughed. "Whose are these . . . ?"

Captain Barry couldn't get over the fantastic evening; he glanced at his watch just before reaching his room, just on two o'clock, that's almost four hours of supreme pleasure he hummed to himself. He had to use the main entrance as the emergency door he left from could only be used from the inside. He fumbled for his keys . . .

Chapter 4

AT SIX-THIRTY THE CLEANING lady arrived to let herself into the officer's mess. Captain Barry picked himself up from the bushes where he had slept on and off for the past four hours; he was cold, tired and very irritable. He raced to the door before it closed saying 'good morning' to the startled woman as he walked casually to his room. "Oh, damn I've locked myself out, could you let me in with your pass key Mrs Wilson?"

John Smith entered the office block five minutes before nine, he had always been punctual; Corporal Jones looked up from his desk. "The captain had to go out early and said for you to clean up your dorm ready for the new inmates, oops, I mean recruits arriving this afternoon. I have to take my wife to the hospital later so perhaps you can see to the poor souls if I'm not back."

"No problem, corporal, is it OK if I go in and get the cleaning stuff."

"Yes, but don't touch anything."

"Sorry, corporal but the door is locked, have you got a key?"

"Yes, there's a spare in the safe, it's a special security lock; quite unusual in shape I don't think there's another like it."

John took the key and unlocked the door then stared at the key for a long time.

"Are you alright, Smith?" The corporal asked.

"Yeah, you're right about the unusual shape. Here you'd better put it back before it gets lost." John carried the bucket of cleaning materials across the road and was almost hit by a three-ton army truck.

"Have you got a death wish, son?" The driver shouted.

John was in a state of shock; it couldn't possibly be him, not Captain Barry but then things began falling into place—the hole in the wall so he could watch the boys in the shower and of course the black eye! 'He got that when our heads bashed together!' He said aloud as he entered his hut, 'and I sucked his cock, shit!'

It was around three o'clock when the first of the new boys arrived, John introduced himself and showed each one around; it made him feel important! Remembering names was going to be a challenge though and the many accents didn't help either! After the last one arrived he called loudly to get their attention then marched them to the quartermasters to collect their kit, from there it was the barber's shop where he watched sad faces gaze at their prized hairstyles lying on the floor. An hour later the squad, dressed in uniform and cropped, unpacked their personal bits from holdalls and suitcases and made their beds. John recognised the footsteps of Captain Barry as he approached. "Stand up straight," recruit Smith bellowed, surprising himself, "squad ready for inspection, sir!" He saluted and the officer returned the compliment.

"Who's in charge?" The abrupt vocal hadn't changed.

"I am, sir, Corporal Jones has taken his wife to the hospital."

The tall officer bent down to my ear level and whispered, "I'm impressed, Smith" then spoke loudly, "listen to me, when myself or Corporal Jones are not around recruit Smith is in charge of this squad, which will be known as squad sixty-three, you will listen and obey. Do as he says or you will feel my wrath. Today's word is discipline; remember that and we'll all get on fine." The officer lowered his head to my level once more, "a word in your ear, outside!"

John's first thoughts were his three day army career was over, insubordination; disrespect to an officer, there must be a thousand things he could be thrown out for.

"Quite honestly I was astonished at the way you took charge. I'm making you acting lance corporal with effect from Monday. It's not all good news though, there's no extra pay and you take the shit when it hits the fan, so my advice is—don't get too friendly with your squad and be strict; further promotion could be just around the corner."

'Why was he being so nice to me,' John thought as he marched his flock to the cookhouse, 'did he know I had his keys?'

His two new friends made space at their table, "has he been in touch?" Pete asked eagerly.

"Who?" John responded.

"The mystery Scotsman, of course!" Ray added.

"There is no mystery Scotsman. I know who he is and if I tell you it must go no further than this table," three heads touched as John told them who owned the keys they found last night.

"What are we going to do?" Pete asked.

"He knows who we are but he doesn't know that we know who he is, does that make sense?"

"I think so." Ray looked baffled.

"I have a plan, it's very dangerous and if we get caught we will, without a doubt be put in gaol and slung out of the army."

Captain Barry opened the office building and caught Corporal Jones just before he was leaving. "Trust your wife is OK, corporal?"

"Yes, thank you sir, she's got another month to go before we have our second child."

"I seem to have mislaid my keys, I don't suppose anybody has handed them in."

"No, sir, but if you need to get into your office there is a spare in the safe, I'll get it for you," he handed over the key.

"You pop off now and I'll see you on Monday."

"Thank you sir, enjoy your weekend."

"When you said dangerous I thought that's what you meant; this is suicidal!" Pete was definitely dubious about the operation.

"I could do it by myself," John was adamant he was going through with it.

"What and let you have all the fun? No way!" Ray laughed, "when shall we do it?"

"How about tonight?"

Captain Barry caught a taxi into town, "Take me to a locksmith, driver, I lost my fucking car keys while out jogging last night, fortunately I wrote the number down in case this ever happened."

"Wouldn't it have been easier to have a spare set cut before you lost them?" The driver answered with a smile.

John made sure his sheep were securely in the pen then met up with his two pals, it was a little after ten. Wearing dark green army overalls, part of their kit, they blackened their faces like commandos and advanced towards their objective. They didn't know in which of the rooms they would find their target but as all accommodation was on one level it shouldn't be too difficult. Most rooms still had lights on which was to their advantage, a darkened room would make it easier to be seen from the inside. John climbed onto Pete's shoulders and peered into the first window and saw two guys playing chess. In the next room, a man in an armchair watching television and in the third was their prey. As John peered through the glass Captain Barry stepped out of the shower and as he dried himself his long cock swayed from side to side. John climbed down from Pete's aching shoulders and whispered, "now we've found him we've got to get in, any suggestions?"

"Yes, let's get the hell out of here before we get caught!" Ray was scared.

"Why not wait for him to go to bed then let ourselves in, you've got a key." Pete was a little braver.

Captain Barry was completely exhausted; he had almost no sleep last night, spent most of the day searching for his keys then having to go into town to get new ones. He was just glad it was Friday; he could spend all the weekend in bed if he wanted. He removed the towel surrounding his waist and hung it over the back of a chair, laid on his bed and switched off the light.

That was their cue to advance; they knew their victim's room was the third on the right from the entrance; John would have to find which, out of the bunch of six keys, would fit the lock. He eliminated the car keys and the captain's office which left three. The outer door was opened with the first of the trio that left two! The hallway was in darkness, the only light coming from underneath doors. The first two were lit which meant the next one was where they should be (or perhaps shouldn't). A door opened filling the hallway with light, the three recruits pinned themselves against the wall motionless as the chess player shouted goodnight to his buddy and disappeared down the corridor; thirty seconds later the light switched off. John fumbled with the key at Captain Barry's door; the first didn't fit but the second did and then they were in. Pete and Ray kept behind their leader who knew the layout, he'd seen it through the window earlier, in the darkness they could easily knock something over and then the game would be finished.

John listened to the regular breathing of their commanding officer; he slowly pulled the sheet covering him and allowed his hand to brush the sleeping flesh. The moonlight was now streaming through the glass onto their goal and the pals of John were sure the ogre would wake from his dreams and gobble them up! The leader placed his hand firmly on the captain's cock and pulled the foreskin down exposing the crown, still no response! Finally, John lifted the heavy flesh and popped it into his mouth; he heard a shocked heavy intake of breath from his two partners in crime, but it had the desired response. The slackness began to harden until it moved into a straight line! Then he stood back. He made both youths take a closer look at the rigid cock; John had placed the key ring over the crown before it had become too hard!

Chapter 5

MORNING CAME AND JOHN, Pete and Ray were up early keeping a close watch on the officer's quarters. It wasn't long before a dark clad figure emerged walking along the road like he had two broken legs, John saluted, "Good morning, sir, are you OK?" He asked politely to the officer in the black tracksuit.

"No, I'm fucking not. I need to get to my office and phone for an ambulance before I die."

As there was nobody about at that time in the day the three recruits assisted the poor man to his office.

"Is it your stomach, sir?" John asked.

"No, it's my fucking cock." He tried to sit in his office chair but yelled in pain.

"Let me have a look!" John pulled down the track suit bottoms revealing the bunch of keys hanging from the end of his still iron hard cock. "Jesus, sir, how did you manage to do that!"

Pete and Ray were biting hard on their lower lips to stop themselves from laughing out loud.

"Have you any wire cutters in your office, sir?" John asked.

"You're not using wire cutters on me; you bastards might cut it off!"

"Well, is there any ice, perhaps if we freeze it?"

"Look, don't fuck about just get me an ambulance."

"It's not going to look good in the local rag when the press gets hold of the story." John was enjoying watching the pain, "Pete go to the cookhouse and get a bag of ice and be quick about it."

In less than a minute the youth returned, John asked his commanding officer to lie across his desk then held the frozen pack against the swelling for a while and gradually the hardness began to shrink.

Ray and Pete gently pushed the ice-cold, soft crown through the ring and handed the set of keys back to its owner.

"Thanks, you were right, it would have looked rather odd taking that to the hospital."

"If you don't mind me asking, sir, how did you do it?" By this time both Ray and Pete had gone to the window to prevent their captain seeing their grinning faces.

"I went to bed last night and when I woke up this morning it was there."

"I hope I'm not speaking out of turn, sir, but perhaps one of the officer's has a grudge against you." Both Pete and Ray stood outside for fear their fuses might blow and bring on hilarious laughter, thus letting the cat out of the bag!

Captain Barry was still holding onto the painful area while lying across his desk.

"Would you like me to make sure it's still working OK, sir?"

"Would you mind, Smith?"

"It would be my pleasure, sir!"

The End

FILTHY WEATHER

.

Chapter 1

DANNY'S MUM'S WEDDING TO Dave went off better than expected, there was always the chance someone would throw a spanner in the works on the second time around. While the taxi whisked them away to the airport for a fortnight honeymooning in Bermuda, Danny completed his plans to go camping by himself in sunny Brighton!

At nine o'clock the sun was shining on a cloudless summer morning, he slung his holdall over his broad shoulders and walked to the main road. 'Not a lot of traffic about at this time of day on a Sunday', went through his mind as he waved a thumb at a passing motorist. He began walking and after a few minutes, a pick-up truck stopped.

"Where you off to, buddy?" The old man asked.

"Brighton."

"I can drop you off at the M23, that's about half way."

"That would be brilliant, thanks."

Steve was preparing the caravan he and Roger bought a year back, a dream four-berth fibreglass beauty complete with awning; everything they needed for a comfortable holiday was loaded into the van along with their two bikes. Roger backed up the 2.8litre Nissan and Steve hooked it up.

"Check the electrics." Roger called and watched the thumbs-up signal in the extended mirrors.

"What are we waiting for; come on, let's go!" Steve smiled excitedly as he climbed in next to his lover.

It had been almost a year since they had been away, their work often prevented holidays together; Roger being in the hotel trade and Steve an aircraft accident investigator. Whenever they planned weekend breaks something often cropped up at the last minute, but this time they were confident every eventuality was covered.

Danny thanked the driver and walked to the slip road of the M23; he couldn't believe his luck when the first vehicle he hailed stopped for him.

"I go to Newhaven, it good for you, yes?" The heavily accented driver called down from his million-wheeled truck. Danny smiled and climbed in; at this rate he'd be at the campsite by lunchtime, he thought. "I from Italy, I speak the good English, yes?"

"If I can understand you then you speak good English!" Danny agreed.

Roger stopped and filled the Nissan with fuel at the local petrol station then it was full speed ahead along the motorway; well, fifty-miles-an-hour! They were in no hurry anyway; just happy to be together.

Steve squeezed his partner's thigh. "Just think, in two hours we'll be sitting under the awning drinking a refreshing beer."

Danny shook hands with the funny truck driver; he'd dropped him off only a few hundred yards from the campsite but as he approached, he could see so many tents and caravans he thought it may be full.

"How many people?" The gateman asked abruptly.

"Just me, I'm by myself." Danny smiled. The man took the boy's money and marked an 'x' on the map; the only available spot.

"Don't get too close to the corner; a caravan will be parking there later today." He warned.

Danny, with map in hand followed the road to the bend and removed the heavy holdall. He had never been camping before; it was Dave, mums new husband, who not only had suggested it but loaned him the tent. He undid the canvass bag and took out the poles and pegs, there were no instructions as to assembling the shelter and he knew he was being watched by the other campers, so he did what most people don't do; he stood up and scratched his head and waited for assistance. Two lads half his age took control and fitted it together in moments then returned to their massive six-berth accommodation. Everything Danny brought with him was in the holdall including a tin of corned beef and plastic fork to eat it with. He was hungry and hot; the sun was blazing from a clear blue sky as it had been for the last two days, he scrambled inside the confines of the canvass, stripped out of his clothes and pulled on his shorts. He found his book in the side pocket of the holdall, ate his meal then relaxed under the sun.

The luxurious Nissan pulled up at the gatehouse, "Good afternoon, gentlemen, have you made a reservation?"

"Yes, I'm Mr Carter, booked in from today for two weeks." Roger informed him politely.

"In that case sir, follow the road to the corner and you'll see the space reserved for you."

The driver backed the van into position, Steve lowered the corner jacks to level it then they fitted the awning between them. In less than ten minutes Roger and Steve were changed into shorts, supping cool beer from a can while relaxing in easy chairs.

Roger, in is early thirties, had almost blond hair, well over six-foot tall, with a sturdy, hairless body. On the other hand Steve was younger, barely twenty-five, he had a dark complexion, not as tall as his friend but built with muscles on top of muscles; he could have been on the front cover of a health magazine!

Danny looked up from his book and watched the two rich guys reclining in their five-star luxury just a few feet away. God, was he envious!

Roger's phone rang. "What? You've got to be joking! I've only just got here." He paused while listening to the other person. "OK, give me a couple of hours."

Steve's worst fears were realised, an emergency at the hotel was dragging his lover away. They had been looking forward to their holiday for months and now it looked like it was ruined before it started. "Come on, let's pack it all up." He said despondently.

"There's no need for both of us to go, half the workforce have contracted food poisoning and I have to organise extra staff for the conference tomorrow. I'll probably be back by Tuesday."

Steve watched as his special friend drove carefully through the grounds and out the gate.

Danny had heard the conversation and felt sorry for them, he'd seen them discreetly hold hands and kiss goodbye in the doorway of the caravan before the older one left in the motor. Each time he looked up from his book he could see the younger man with his face in his hands, he looked so sad! The sun was low in the sky and a gentle breeze blew in off the sea, it was refreshing after the day's heat. Danny grabbed his towel and bar of soap then traipsed down to the toilet block to take a shower. The queue was long; there were only three showers and probably a dozen bodies waiting to be washed. He was in no hurry and waited patiently. The man from the caravan stood behind him in line; Danny smiled but received little response in return.

Steve was full of rage, the last time they had arranged to go away for a weekend there had been a helicopter crash and he'd been ordered to investigate the cause. Something always cropped up and it seemed so unfair. He washed himself and dried the same time as Danny, this time he did take notice of the fair-haired naked youth standing close to him. He waited until the muscled teenager was finished then followed a few steps behind to see where he was camped. A smile crept across his face when he saw how close the good looking boy was to his van.

It was becoming dark too early, thick black clouds appeared on the horizon before the sun had set and the wind was getting stronger. People began lashing down lightweight furniture and closing up zips. Using the mallet, Danny knocked the tent pegs hard into the ground to make sure he didn't get blown away then unrolled his sleeping bag and crawled onto it; he turned on his torch and continued reading his novel as the wind became stronger. He didn't remember falling asleep but water dripping on his face woke him. The heavens had opened up; the rain was torrential and coming in everywhere. He cursed Dave for lending him a leaky tent! The beam from his torch showed just how dire his situation was; if his half read book was floating in his sleeping bag there wouldn't be a dry spot anywhere. His heart missed a beat when he heard the zip being opened on his tent.

"I think you may need rescuing!" The smiling face said in the torchlight. "Leave everything here until morning and hurry I'm getting soaked!"

Danny followed the figure to the caravan nearby then realised who it was. "Thanks, I could have drowned in there!"

They stood for a few minutes under the awning watching the teeming rain tipping out of the clouds. "They say three fine days and a thunderstorm so I supposed it's expected. My name's Steve, by the way."

"And I'm Danny."

"Let's go inside, it's warmer in there." They climbed the two steps and into luxury. Danny's shorts were stuck to his body and he shivered even though it wasn't cold. Steve drew the curtains, "Take those off and dry yourself with a towel before you catch pneumonia." He picked up the wet garment, wrung out the rainwater over the sink then hung it above the cooker. "It'll be dry by the morning." He said while towelling his own body.

Danny wrapped the towel around his waist and apologised for making the floor wet with his bare feet. "Why don't you sit by the window and let me worry about that. What do you fancy, whisky or brandy?"

"I think a little brandy will go down nicely, thank you."

"You are old enough to drink, aren't you? I don't want your dad knocking on my door." He joked.

"I'm nineteen and my dad's dead."

"Oh, I'm sorry Danny, I'm always putting my big foot in my mouth."

"You weren't to know, he had cancer and passed away three years ago. Mum's just got married again, in fact they are on honeymoon now and I bet it's not raining in Bermuda." They both laughed then looked deep into each other's eyes. Danny had always known he was different, he'd even told his mum but Dave was another matter, probably that's why they didn't get on.

"I haven't seen my dad since my twenty-first birthday, that's when Roger and me came out; we told everyone at the party, they all cheered and clapped except my father, he walked out on mum and me and I've not seen him since; my parents are divorced now." Steve picked up his tumbler, smiled again and said cheers; they touched glasses. It was obvious Danny was tired, he'd been up early, walked more than a few miles with a heavy burden and been disturbed from his dreams, "maybe we should turn in," he suggested, "I hope you don't mind sharing." The sleepy-eyed backpacker just smiled.

Danny removed his towel and crawled across the double size bed; he was against the wall. Steve studied the round white cheeks contrasting with the sun-tanned body before turning off the light then removed his shorts; he didn't want the boy to see his erection! "Are you comfortable?"

"I think you know the answer to that after the hard ground I was lying on outside," he giggled.

Steve climbed in and pulled the covers over both of them, then rested a hand on the pretty youth's thigh, "you're cold, let me warm you."

With his eyes closed, Danny felt the warm hand at the top of his leg moving gently to and fro; a second hand joined the first slowly moving in unison gradually getting closer to his balls.

The sensitive fingers of the dark skinned man made contact with the ball bag as if by accident, "sorry!" he apologised in a whisper.

"That's ok!" Danny had a hard on pointing to his stomach, thus when the warming hands moved to his chest he guessed it would only be seconds before it was noticed. He had never had a sexual experience with anyone other than his right hand and was enjoying the thrill of being touched but at the same time wary of what could happen to him. Everyone had heard stories of the crazed axe man who chops his victims up after having his evil way with them!

Steve's palms slid delicately over the smooth chest, caressing the spiked nipples and listening to laboured breathing, "are you ok with this?"

"It feels good."

The stomach muscles were like steel as Steve's hands roamed so very slowly over taut flesh; contact! The little finger of his right hand touched the hardness of the youth's cock, moved away slightly then reached it a second time resting the small finger onto the hot helmet, "can I suck it?" Another whisper reached Danny's ears in the darkness.

"I don't mind," he'd never been sucked before so he didn't know what it involved but had a pretty good idea.

When Steve was given the green light he went down on the boy in a flash before he changed his mind, unaware it was his first time! He greedily swallowed the stem until his nose embedded itself in soft curly hair.

Nothing before in his short life could have prepared him for the wet lips descending on his seven-inch pole. The sensation made his body fold in two; his head left the pillow and his feet rose in the air as the tongue travelled swiftly up and down his column at the speed of light. "Stop!" He shouted above the noise of the rain hitting the van roof.

Hands gripped tightly on either side of Steve's face lifting him off, "you don't like it?"

"I'm loving it, but you're going too fast and I don't want to cum yet."

The mouth went back over the rock-hard cock and continued thrilling Danny at half speed! The young man couldn't believe his luck, with Roger back at the hotel he thought he would be spending the night on his own; the horrendous weather had done him a big favour!

Roger drove into the hotel car park using his reserved space; he walked through reception to the staff quarters where Jeff was waiting. "What took you so long, I've missed you!"

The hotel manager looked into the teenager's tearful eyes, "I'm sorry, my love, the traffic was at a crawl because of this awful weather. Let's go to my room."

Jeff was a waiter and apart from being very pretty was good at his job. Roger put him in charge of the main bar where he entertained the customers with his 'tossing bottles' routine while mixing cocktails. His beautiful smile and blue eyes drew scores of young girls ordering drinks they didn't really want but the bar takings were up from the day he took over. Jeff was gay and it didn't take Roger long to find out. He and Jeff were clearing up after a lively wedding reception one Saturday in May, Roger changed a barrel of lager and as Jeff pulled the tap he received a shower of cold beer, he removed his soaked shirt and Roger used a tea-towel to dry his chest and stomach; Jeff's nipples went hard as the manager's hands touched his skin, they gazed into each other's eyes and the deal was done.

Tonight's meeting had been arranged by Roger earlier in the week, a hoax call to bring him back and into his lover's heart. They stripped and lay naked on the bed locked in each other's arms. "Who would you like me to be tonight?" Jeff wanted to know.

"You can be the schoolmaster and I'll be the naughty pupil, you know where the toys are!" He switched off the light.

Danny's muscular frame trembled under slurping lips, every up and down movement brought a new thrill to his excited body causing his heart to miss a beat and those fingers, those gentle sensitive fingers creeping over his skin, he thought in his mind he had drowned in the tent and gone to heaven. The head lifted from his crotch and Steve kneeled between the panting youth's wide open legs.

"Would you do it to me?"

"I'll try, I've never done it before!"

Steve threw the bed covers to the floor then pulled Danny by the ankles into the centre of the mattress; he climbed back turning the opposite way and allowed the camper's fumbling fingers to locate his solid throbbing cock. A sigh emitted through open lips as two soft hands gripped firmly around his shaft and then hot breath, a second before a solitary slow lick over his crown, further action by the tongue was causing Steve to moan loudly.

Danny opened his lips fully to accommodate the bulbous head, the monster cock was so fat and long that was all he could get inside his mouth. The twenty-five-year-old had not enjoyed sex this much since his first time with Roger who taught him everything he knew. His mouth went back to sucking Danny with renewed vigour, his mind flashing between his new young conquest and his older companion.

Danny was getting used to the job, the clean, musky smell of soap filled his nostrils and he began copying every pleasurable move. When his balls were gently squeezed he applied equal pressure to those in his hands, when tickling fingers touched his stomach he repeated the action but when the mouth sunk down to his pubic hair he almost gagged and he heard Steve laugh. The novice lifted his head, "am I doing it right?"

"You're doing it perfectly!"

Roger was shackled face down to the bed, wrists and ankles secured with rubber handcuffs to each corner, Jeff stood above him with a long, fine cane. "I've told you a thousand times about jerking off in class, tonight you will be punished severely for disobeying me!" The thin stick swished through the air before landing on Roger's bare cheeks; he yelled at the unexpected ferocity warning his torturer not to leave any scars. The lad took a towel from the bathroom, laid it across his victims arse and hit him even harder several times. "That's for being late but this one is 'cause I love you!" He discarded the towel and began kissing the rounded bum cheeks. The tickling sensation was too much for Roger and he tried to close his legs together, forgetting they were tethered wide open. The kissing turned to licking and the boy's tongue slid slowly down the crack until reaching the furry hole. Forcing the two mounds further apart he easily forced his wet, searching tongue deep inside the cavity. Roger's finger's dug into the pillow and his toes curled with the fantastic sensation, this was a first and it had taken an eighteen-year-old to give him the most pleasurable experience of his life.

Jeff freed his new friend and, after massaging his joints, sat on the bed, "I know you enjoyed that 'cause you almost sucked all my tongue into your arsehole," they both laughed, "I could do that for you every day if you get rid of Steve."

"We've been over this a dozen times or more, Steve and me have been together for over ten years, he was still at school when I met him, we live in a house together, have investments; I can't just walk away from him like that."

"But I love you, Roger, does Steve?"

"Of course he does, I feel sorry for him sleeping in that caravan all by himself while I'm cuddled up to you, he'd never dream of going with anybody else!"

Danny and Steve had been sucking each other for over an hour but time had stood still for them; even their loud moans and sighs of joy would be mistaken for the wind by the neighbours.

Chapter 2

It was still overcast in the morning but the rain had ceased as the young camper sat up peering through the curtain. He looked down at the heaving wide chest of the man who had given him the most pleasurable night of his life. The spiky nipples were tempting to touch but something more urgent was on his mind—he needed a piss real bad! He tried unsuccessfully to climb from the bed without waking the handsome man; a hand went between his legs grabbing a firm hold on his cock and balls, "you're not leaving me, are you?" Steve smiled.

"I need a pee!" Danny smiled back, "and if you keep holding it I'll do it on the floor!"

"Behind the door you'll find a bucket, do it in there and I'll empty it later." Steve listened to the fast stream hitting the side of the plastic container and his cock became hard again, he turned onto his front. Touching his gigantic cock in the darkness was one thing but seeing it in broad daylight was something else and he had plans for his third eye to visit virgin territory very soon.

"Thanks for last night, Steve, I've never enjoyed myself so much." He knelt down beside the bed, leaned forward and kissed his new friend's cheek.

"There's more to learn and I can teach you." He said softly looking into beautiful light blue eyes.

"What about your friend?"

"He said he wouldn't be back until tomorrow. I'll tell you what, I'll prepare breakfast for the two of us while you dismantle your tent and bring it into the awning to dry then we'll decide what to do for the rest of the day and if you want to learn more we can have an early night, say about six o'clock." They both laughed.

Jeff released himself from Roger's tight grip, they had fallen asleep, their limbs intertwined. The young waiter stared onto the closed eyes of the man almost twice his age; he wanted to be Roger's number one more than anything in the world and was determined to win his war against Steve no matter what the price. He had to think of a scheme to undermine the dark skinned bodybuilder so that he could take his place.

Danny hung his sleeping bag next to the opening of the awning; the breeze would soon dry the saturated material. He glanced around the field watching disappointed holidaymakers sweeping water from their tents and waved to the two boys who had helped erect his, they returned his wave but the sadness on their faces sent a feeling of depression through him. "Breakfast is served!" The voice startled him.

"That could be me wringing out my clothes if you hadn't saved me last night."

"And I could have slept all alone and by myself. But I'm glad I didn't, Danny. I had one of the best nights in my life, thanks to you," he whispered.

With breakfast over Steve suggested a bike ride into town.

Roger took a shower with his sweetheart; they lathered each other in bubbles, kissed, touched and when he was ready, Jeff turned facing the wall, he used his hands for support and his feet wide apart waiting for his boss to fuck him. Roger spread shower gel liberally over his circumcised cock and guided the purple crown against the smooth hole; he listened to the moans of the boy pressed against the shower wall as he thrust his hard pole into the warm cave until skin touched skin. As soon as Jeff clenched his bum cheeks together Roger wrapped his arms around the youth's chest and tweaked his nipples. The in and out movement built into a rhythm, synchronising a pace which was comfortable to them both until Roger let out a warning to his boyfriend, "I'm coming, my love!" That was a signal for Jeff to release and clench his cheeks in quick succession over and over until his lover had finished his orgasm, "Oh, baby, you certainly know what I like!"

"And there's plenty more where that came from—just say the word and I'll move in with you!"

"Please don't start that again, Jeff. Why can't you be satisfied with what we have?"

"Because I have nothing, I get you when you want. It doesn't matter that I want you twenty-four hours a day. You have that other guy in your bed when it should be me!"

"Now, now, settle down, we don't want a drama. When this happened the first time in the bar after the wedding I had no idea we would become so involved. Perhaps we should cool it down a little, you know, see each other less often."

"No way—you started this by giving me a wank in the bar, remember? I didn't ask you to do it."

"You are being immature; I've given most of the waiters a wank at some time or another." Roger laughed.

"Oh, is that all I am now, a fucking waiter? What happened to the lovey-dovey sweet talk in bed while you're fucking me?"

"I think I'll get dressed and leave and you should do the same, what time does your shift begin?"

"Is work all you can think about? Perhaps I should tell your precious Steve what we've been doing."

"You don't have to do that, I shall tell him myself and you can look for another job!" With that, Roger waited for the sulking youth to dress then escorted him to the hotel entrance, telling the security guard not to let him back in.

Jeff knew Steve was in Brighton waiting for his other half to return, if he could alert him Roger had been fooling around with a waiter in the hotel it could be the end of their relationship. Out of sight of the guard, he went to the back of the hotel where he knew the kitchen door was always open, from there he walked confidently to Roger's office, nobody would take any notice if they saw him entering, he was doing it all the time. The top drawer contained the phone book; he searched the index for 'S' and found the mobile number at the top of the page and dialled.

"Hello?" A voice answered.

"Is that Steve?"

"No, it's a friend, can I take a message?"

Jeff was stunned; he hadn't planned for someone else answering the phone. "Yes, tell him his lover boy, Roger, has been screwing around with a hotel waiter for the past three months."

"Whom shall I say called?" The phone went dead.

Steve emerged from the bank clutching a fistful of notes from the hole-in-the-wall machine. "Was that my phone?"

"Yes, it was someone trying to sell double-glazing. But I told them you weren't interested." He lied.

"Good for you." He smiled. The sun came out and it was warm as they approached the beach. "Fancy a swim?"

"We haven't bought any gear."

"It's a nudie beach, we don't need any!" Steve chained and locked the bikes to a lamppost then they walked over the huge pebbles until they were close to the water. "You go in first while I look after the stuff. I don't want some thief running off with my money."

Danny stripped off then ran into the water, swam half a dozen strokes then came out. "Jesus, that's cold!"

"You'll soon dry in the sun; I just wish I could cuddle you to warm you up."

"Don't say things like that I'll get a hard-on again."

Steve dropped his shorts, it was the first time Danny had seen him fully naked and in the upright position. He was looking at a picture of beauty; the muscular body was a sight to behold, all eyes for miles around gazed at the Adonis as he strolled into the sea.

"Is that Steve?" A voice said over Danny's shoulder.

"Yes."

"I haven't seen him for a couple of years, is he not with Roger anymore?" The stranger asked.

"They are on holiday together in their caravan but Roger had to go back to his hotel."

"Here, sit on my blanket and use my towel to dry yourself. Are you wearing sun cream?"

"No, I didn't bring any with me."

"Lay down and I'll spread some over you, the sun can be quite dangerous, you know." Oil squirted from a bottle over Danny's chest and was softly rubbed into his skin. One arm then the other, the left leg and the right and then it was the turn of the stomach; a hand moved very slowly in circles, lower and lower until it reached the hairline. Danny tried to concentrate on something else but to no avail, a little finger was at the base of his cock, his balls began to contract as blood pumped into his slack flesh and in an instant he felt it slap against his belly. "Well, hello Nobby!" The stranger said as his greasy hand clasped the pulsating cock drenching it in the slippery sun block."

"Is that you, Dave?" Danny sat up covering his erection with his hands on hearing Steve's voice.

"It certainly is my good friend."

"What are you doing in this part of the world?" He shook the water from his cropped hair.

"Why, I live here, just across the road, actually. I bought a hotel, exclusively gay of course, you can see it from here, the one with the rainbow logo on the roof."

"Very subtle, we'll have to look you up, we're here for a couple of weeks."

"Who's we?" Dave asked looking at Danny.

"Oh, I'm sorry, Danny this is Dave an old friend from my schooldays." They shook hands. "I rescued Danny from his tent last night, wasn't that a dreadful storm." Dave's eyes were glued to Danny's gorgeous body and half-hard cock. "I'm expecting Roger back tomorrow; he got called back to work, something about food poisoning."

"Someone's been trying to phone you; it rings once then cuts out." Danny passed the phone to Steve.

"That often happens on the beach, we're too low for the signal; you will have to go up to the road if you want to make a call." Dave advised.

"That's Roger's number, I'd better find out what he wants." He pulled on his shorts over wet skin, highlighting his manhood.

"And how did you get here my pretty young man?"

Danny recited the story of his mum getting married, hitch-hiking to the camp site and Steve saving him from the storm. He didn't go into detail of his sexual adventure.

"And where will you be sleeping tonight?"

"In my tent, I suppose."

"You know another storm's been forecast, don't you?"

"Oh, don't say that, my tent leaks like a sieve."

"I've had a cancellation at my place, you're quite welcome to stay there."

"Sorry, but my budget doesn't allow me any luxuries."

"The room was paid for in advance, it's yours for a few days if you want it."

"Thanks, I appreciate that, perhaps I can do something to repay your kindness."

"I'm pretty sure I will think of something."

"That was Roger," Steve returned from making his call, "he's on his way back, should be here in an hour. I think we'd better go he sounded worried."

"I'll see you later, Dave." Danny shook hands with Dave again. The two cycles were unlocked and Steve and Danny rode slowly back to the campsite.

"It's going to be a bit awkward explaining to Roger that you stayed last night."

"Why say anything, I'll rig my tent up when I get back, Dave said I could stay in the hotel for a few days until this weather sorts itself out."

"Thanks Danny, Roger sounded strange, almost in tears, I hope he's alright."

"Be honest with each other, don't have secrets. Dave has seen us together and if you meet up with him again something may innocently slip out."

"Jesus, you're such a nice guy, Danny. I would never have thought of that."

Danny fixed his tent, the sleeping bag was dry as was most of his stuff in the holdall except for his book, he would never know 'who done it'.

Danny borrowed a small bag from Steve, he stuffed it with clean underwear and toiletries then walked away from his tent but something made him look back.

Steve waved to the youth from the awning then disappeared back inside his van, he looked through the window at the empty tent and a tear ran down his cheek. "I think I'm falling in love again," he said to himself.

The young camper walked to the seafront, past tall Victorian buildings until he came to the 'Rendezvous' hotel. He pressed the bell and was pleasantly surprised when a youth wrapped only in a towel opened the door; their smiles greeted each other before a word was spoken. "You must be Danny, Dave's description said you were pretty but that was an understatement you're fucking gorgeous, come in and take your clothes off. By the way I'm Adrian also known as the butler."

Danny was more than a little taken aback by the doorman's outspokenness but followed him inside anyway. "You leave your clothes and things in your room which is just down the hall," he flung open the door for Danny to see, "take a shower, there's the most delightful smelling gel in your bathroom and then join us in the lounge. Only towels or less may be worn once you are past the welcome mat. Enjoy your stay!" He leaned forward and kissed the cheek of the embarrassed country-boy.

Roger pulled up between the van and a frail looking tent, he'd had time to reflect on what he'd been up to over the last few months. If he said nothing it would always be on his conscience but if he told the truth would he be forgiven? He decided to continue with the lie, for now, anyway!

"Welcome back, you had me worried you sounded so sad on the phone is everything all right?"

"I'm probably tired, we had a late night and early morning and you know how grumpy I get if I don't get my six hours."

"I'll make you a nice cup of tea while you get undressed, we can sit under the awning and you can tell me all about the drama!"

"What do you mean by 'the drama'?" Roger looked shocked that he should know.

"The emergency, of course, what you had to go back for!"

"Oh, that! I called the recruitment office and they sent some people round."

"But they don't open on Sundays."

"I don't know, let's just say it's sorted and leave it at that!"

Steve watched as his partner lay on the bed in the same place Danny had been a few hours earlier. Why did Roger have to come back so soon and spoil the fun?

There was no denying Danny felt self-conscious walking into the lounge wearing only a towel, it barely came to the top of his thigh and he knew if he bent down it would give everyone a good view of his hole! The room fell into silence as the dozen or so guests gazed in awe at the beauty making a discrete entrance. His eyes flashed from one to the next in the hope he would see Dave or Adrian but neither were there.

"Come over and sit opposite me and tell us who you are." One guest smiled.

'Yes, so you can look up inside my towel,' went through Danny's mind. He smiled and began telling how the rain had washed him out of his tent last night, however someone else had a similar story and interrupted with their tale of woe. He studied the face of the storyteller then each one of the audience. There was nobody in the room he could compare with Steve, every time a picture of the quiet man's face appeared in his mind his stomach knotted and he felt sad enough to cry. Why did he feel this way for someone he hardly knew?

Roger was in a bad mood and Steve didn't know the reason, every time he tried to make conversation the older man bit his head off. "Look, Roger, I don't know why you're being so nasty to me; if you think I've done something wrong tell me," a pause of silence followed, "I think I'll go for a walk, perhaps you'll like me a little better when I return." Steve never raised his voice, even when Roger ranted and raved over some trivial disagreement, Steve kept his cool which seemed to annoy Roger even more! The young man walked to the promenade, watching the incoming tide; the waves relaxed him and his mind wandered to the events of last night and, as if someone was calling his name, his head turned towards Dave's hotel where he knew the boy was staying.

"Why, hello stranger! Boy, are you good looking! Unfortunately the hotel is full . . ."

"OK, Adrian, this is Steve, he's a friend of mine." Dave butted in. "Come on in, we'll go to my room it's a little more private there." Dave poured two brandies, "you see,

I even remember what you drink. Now, tell me, what have you and Roger been doing since I saw you last year?"

"We seem to be falling apart," Steve began.

"Never! You two are an institution; you've been together for ten years."

"I feel it's all over between us, I get the impression he's seeing someone else. The phone calls he takes in private, late nights at the hotel and now this story about the staff having food poisoning, it just doesn't add up. I'm so depressed I just want to go home and get back to work."

"What about the boy I saw you with at the beach, Danny I think he said his name was?"

"He took up your offer and should be here somewhere in the hotel."

Dave pressed the intercom button on his desk, "Adrian, has Danny arrived yet?" a short pause, "ok bring him to my office, please."

The door opened and Danny's heart melted at the sight of Steve, he literally ran into his arms trying to squeeze the life out of him; Steve held him tightly.

"Right then, I had better see to my other guests." Dave felt awkward and excused himself.

The two strangers from yesterday seemed to spend an eon staring into each other's eyes, conveying messages only they understood, the mutual feeling of need for each other; their grip tightening until it hurt.

The quiet man held the camper's shoulder's at a distance and whispered. "I love you, Danny."

It took all of a millisecond for the boy to realize the feelings he'd been having all day and tears formed in both his eyes. "I think I love you too!" They hugged, squeezed and kissed until Dave reappeared.

"My god, are you two still at it. Take him to your room, Danny so I can get some work done."

A picture of a smiling James Dean hung over the bed as Steve removed his clothes. Danny sat on the bed watching the 'he-man' drop his undershorts, "wow, it looks a lot bigger than it did this afternoon."

"That cold water made it shrivel to half size," he laughed, then noticed a small basket on the bedside table containing condoms and lubrication, "how would you like me to excite you even more than last night," he wrapped his arms around the boy and kissed his moist lips.

"If it pleases you, you can do whatever you want with me as long as it doesn't hurt."

"I could never hurt you, Danny. I want you to be part of my life." Steve tore at the packet then fitted the rubber over the expanding crown, watched curiously by his young conquest.

"Are you sure this isn't going to hurt, I mean, my hole is so small," he said aloud, then to himself, 'but it won't be if that goes inside me.'

"Lay on your back, now lift your legs onto my shoulders," he squeezed some jelly onto his fingers and lubricated the virgin cavity, Danny closed his eyes and murmured, then some more was spread along the length of the huge portion of cock. "Relax, and listen to my voice; the head of my penis is against your back passage and as I ease forward you will feel it enter you, for your own comfort and mine you must remain relaxed." It had breached the barricade without him realizing it; the smooth voice had done the trick. Steve moved with such gentleness, Danny never made a sound; their eyes did all the talking. Steve passed his love for the boy in his mind and Danny received it. The whole length had reached its goal and the smiling man's pubic hair touched the youth's smooth balls, he pulled back so very slowly, an inch at the time and then down again. The action was repeated over and over, the speed increasing with each thrust.

Danny watched the muscles change shape, the veins protrude and the perspiration appear on the kind face above him. He began squeezing his cheeks together on the up stroke and releasing on the down, bringing a further smile to the man on top.

"Wank yourself, Danny, I'm almost there!"

The youth obliged, coming first, and as he did, clenched his cheeks so tight Steve called out and convulsed while pumping fluid into the rubber sock. He collapsed onto Danny's sweat covered body smothering him in kisses.

"Thanks Steve, that was wonderful, even better than what we did last night. Will you stay with me tonight?

"I want to stay with you forever!"

Roger was getting really mad, where was Steve? Why hadn't he come back? He looked at the clock for the thousandth time; it was almost midnight, then his phone rang. "What do *you* want?"

"I want to apologize for calling Steve, I know I shouldn't have but . . ."

"You did what?"

"I was upset that you didn't want to see me again."

"I didn't say that, I said you couldn't move in with me. Look I'm sorry I lost my temper with you; your job is safe and I'll see you when I've finished my holiday."

"I love you, Roger!"

"Yeah, ok, I love you too."

"Won't Roger worry if you don't go back tonight?"

"Probably, he was in a foul mood that's why I searched for you. I stood watching the waves and heard you calling my name as they broke on the pebbles."

"You're so romantic, Steve. You have the most sensitive voice of anyone I know."

"And you have the bluest eyes, the most beautiful smile, the cheekiest laugh, I could go on forever."

After a long pause Danny sat up and stroked the cropped hair of the young man who had given him so much pleasure. "I'm not going to see you after tonight, am I?"

"I don't know, Roger and myself have been together for a long time but we've been drifting apart especially over the last few months. I have my suspicions that he's been seeing someone."

"He has!"

"What? How do you know?" He sat up with such a start he almost knocked Danny off the bed.

"That call I answered when you was at the bank was from a guy saying Roger was fooling around with a waiter from the hotel."

"You should have told me before."

"I thought it would upset you and spoil your day."

"It may have and then I wouldn't be with you now."

Roger dialled Jeff's mobile, "yes?"

"Did I wake you?"

"Oh, Roger, how sweet of you to call, I've been crying most of the evening thinking I've upset you!"

"I'm coming back tonight, I'll get a taxi. Meet me at the hotel in a couple of hours and we'll talk again about living together."

"Oh, you've made me feel like a new man, thank you my darling, I'm sending a trail of kisses down the line."

"It's a mobile, Jeff, there is no line."

"I'll send them via the nearest satellite then."

Roger scribbled a note explaining his love for the hotel barman and apologized for not coming clean about it sooner. 'I've not fallen out of love with you, Steve, I just feel I'm in a rut and need a change. Please forgive me but don't forget the good times we had. We'll sort out the financial arrangements when you come home after your holiday.' He signed it leaving a single 'x' at the bottom then placed the teapot on it.

He walked to the main road and found a taxi waiting outside the Rendezvous hotel.

Chapter 3

S<small>TEVE</small> <small>WOKE</small> <small>FIRST</small> <small>AND</small> peered down at the sleeping beauty, his blemish-free skin had caught the sun yesterday enhancing his good looks. The bed sheet covered his legs and came almost to his waist exposing his powerful chest and narrow waist and the golden pubic hair. He would have to give this Adonis up to go back to Roger; or would he? If his lover of ten years can see someone on the side why shouldn't he? 'I'll go back and confront him about this waiter and see what he says!' He was still working on his plan when the boy opened his eyes. "I can't think of a better way of waking up than seeing you by my side."

"You should be a poet, you dream up the nicest things to say." Danny's grin disappeared as he saw Steve struggling with something to say.

"I have made a decision, Danny, I'm leaving Roger. If you want we can live together or if you don't, we can still see each other. You see, I've fallen head over heels in love with you and I don't want to live without you."

"I didn't know what love was until yesterday, you made me so happy, not just the sexual things we did together but you radiate happiness with your smile. You made me feel wanted."

"And I want you more than you will ever know. Come on, get dressed. Let's get over to Roger and confront him.

Don't be frightened, he may shout and scream but he's never violent.

A few people were about in the caravan park but most were still in their beds or sleeping bags; it was just before eight o'clock. Steve used his key to open the door and walked inside. He instantly saw the note and read it. "You were right, Danny, he is seeing somebody else and he's gone back to him. At least he's left us the car to tow the van back. What part of the country do you come from?"

"I live in a little village in Kent."

"That's a coincidence, which one? I live in Kent as well."

"Cliffe, it's between the River Thames . . ."

"And the River Medway. I live three miles down the road from you. We've probably passed each other in Woolworth's." They both laughed. "Are you working, at college or one of the thousands of unemployed?"

"I've been offered a job by the local council. I've just finished three years at college, learning to be a landscape gardener like my dad." He looked deeply into Steve's smiling eyes again, "it was just before he died when I told mum I was gay she said one day I would find a man to make me happy and she was right."

The next few days were cloudy and miserable but not for Steve and Danny, it was an opportunity to get to know each other; while holidaymakers wore wellingtons, as well as long sad faces, the pair were full of smiles and happiness.

Twelve days passed since Roger left and it was time for Steve to get back, the van was hooked up and Danny collected his sticks and canvas before sitting in the most luxurious motor ever. They approached the Medway towns, familiar landmarks raced by and a feeling of depression hit both at the same time. "What do you think Roger will say when he sees me?"

"I really don't know, he hasn't made contact since he walked out although I left him a couple of messages warning him of our arrival."

"You told him about me already?"

"If he thinks I've found someone to love maybe it will ease his conscience."

"I think there's still a piece of him left in your heart." Danny smiled at the driver.

"Perhaps a little, but not as much as there is for you!"

The old secluded house stood in its own grounds surrounded by tall trees, making it invisible from the road. Steve backed the van into a wooden barn and switched off the motor. The house was completely quiet not even the sound of a bird broke the silence; Steve opened the door and called, "Roger, are you at home?" No response. Another note explaining he and Jeff had moved into the hotel was left in a prominent position under a vase on the table. "It looks like we've got the place to ourselves." They hugged and kissed, "come on I'll show you around." Danny was gob smacked at the size of the place and the beautiful gardens. "We've even got our own wishing well so there's never a shortage of water for the grounds. How would you like to be my landscape gardener and house boy?"

Danny's eyes filled with tears of happiness, "I'd love to do both, Steve, thanks. But can I go round to my place and see mum and Dave, they should be back from their honeymoon by now and I need to collect some stuff?"

"What, like your teddy bear?" He laughed.

"I don't need a teddy bear to cuddle up to at night anymore, do I?" They jumped in the Nissan and ten minutes later were at Danny's mum's place. "I want you to meet her, she's real nice and I know she'll like you."

They entered through the back door, Danny's mum was washing the dishes and Dave was drying.

"Hi mum I'm back from Brighton and I've brought a friend with me," she looked up and smiled while reaching for a towel to dry her wet hands.

Dave turned, "Steve?"

Steve looked up, "dad?"

The End

RETRIBUTION

Chapter 1

Tommy Fletcher climbed out of the cool water and up the rocks, he laughed as his pursuing friend Daniel slipped and cursed, Tommy was a much stronger swimmer, learning to survive the treacherous sea after falling from a wall when just three-years-old.

The two naked youths eased the wooden planks away from the derelict old storehouse door and moments later were inside their secret place. Tommy ran to the corner illuminated with a beam of sunlight and lay on a raised pile of discarded sacks and rags. The heat from the warm rays excited Tommy, his spread-eagled, muscular frame was sporting an erection by the time his pal had refitted the panel. Daniel flexed his own muscles and waved his half hard cock to and fro before covering his long-time friend with his body. "I thought you were going to do it to me." The boy on top whispered between kisses.

"I did it to you yesterday!"

"Yes, but you came too quickly, it only lasted a few minutes."

"You put it up me first and if I've got any strength left I'll fuck you, but you'll have to suck it first."

"I'll do that anyway." The smiling boy whispered again as Tommy lifted his legs high into the air and began pulling on his seven-inch cock. Daniel spat into his hand then spread the saliva around his bulbous crown and placed it against the orifice; he eased forward slowly, and watching the expression on his lovers face, inched forward until his balls swung against Tommy's arse cheeks.

The graceful rhythm of Daniel's bum moving to and fro was being observed by Matthew Quintal, like the two boys performing just a few feet below, all three were apprentices at the old wood shop in Plymouth. But in contrast to his workmates he had a jealous streak as far as Tommy was concerned, he wanted to take Tommy's place as Daniel's friend, he yearned for the opportunity to be fucked by the good-looking youth who had always rejected him as an equal. Wherever Tommy and Daniel played he was always around and they had to think of devious ways to be alone so they could do what they were doing now.

In the days of sail, carpentry was the main trade in the old town, with so many of the king's ships in and out of port every day there was an abundance of work for the townspeople and this week was special; both Tommy and Daniel celebrated their eighteenth birthday within two days of each other and as a surprise their fathers set up a business for them. Matthew Quintal was outraged when he found out he wasn't included in their enterprise; he was intent on bringing to nought their plans by any means possible.

Daniel Winterbottom pumped his cock into Tommy's bum at high speed, wanting to finish quickly, wanting it to be his turn; his face broke into a grin as he looked at the smiling face beneath him. "What's going on in your mind?"

"If you keep wanking my cock like that, I'll come and won't have any left for you!" Daniel released his grip on the swollen pole in an instant and they both laughed.

In the rafters above, Matthew Quintal eyed the lovers through a wide crack in the boards, he began pulling furiously on his enormous meat, it was easily two inches longer than Tommy Fletcher's and fatter as well; he could certainly satisfy the gorgeous Daniel much better than his rival.

"I'm coming, Tommy!" Sweat poured onto the boy below from Daniel's soaked body as he withdrew his wilting stem.

"It's shrivelling up," Tommy laughed as he lowered his feet.

"That's 'cause I've got nothing to keep it up anymore, perhaps if you put your lips around it, the creases will disappear." They both laughed again. They were happy and content with their lives but most of all they were in love.

The immature Matthew Quintal was a year senior to the lovers who were changing position, he preferred watching when Tommy was on top, he could look down into Daniel's eyes and imagine it was himself fucking the arse off the pretty boy.

"You're not going to hurt me, are you?" Daniel asked quietly.

"Not unless my cock has grown another six inches overnight, I think if a horse fucked your arse you'd enjoy it," was Tommy's reply.

"Don't put ideas like that in my mind, I saw that Matthew Quintal taking a piss the other day, I've never seen a cock that big on anyone. Now, I wouldn't mind that going up inside me!" He giggled.

Those few words made Matthew Quintal's eyes almost pop from his head and his hand race faster on his cock; it also made him even more determined to get rid of his rival one way or another.

Tommy took it slow and easy, giving his friend as much pleasure as he had received; they gazed into each other's eyes, conveying their feelings with unspoken words, no two friends had loved more than Tommy and Daniel and the thought of ever being separated never entered their minds. "Start jacking yourself off, Danny, I'm almost there. Oh! Here it comes!" He pulled out, finishing it by hand and squirting streams of his milk over Daniel's chest and stomach.

"I wish you wouldn't do that, I'll have to go for a swim to get it off."

"We've got to collect our clothes from behind the rocks so you'd get your feet wet anyway; just let me be in front when you dive in; I don't want to get a mouthful of that stuff even if it is mine!" He laughed. After carefully removing the planks Tommy pushed his friend through the gap by sticking a finger up his arse making him holler, but just as Tommy squeezed his wide shoulders into the space he heard a sound behind him; he waited momentarily.

"What's the matter?" Daniel asked.

"I thought I heard something."

"It was probably just a bird, come on, this stuff is turning to glue."

Matthew Quintal had wanked five times that afternoon; he had bit his lip to stop himself from crying out with excitement, except for the last time! He had moaned too loudly and he knew Tommy had heard him. But that wouldn't matter if the scheming plan he had in his mind came to fruit. He had found a different way in and out of the storehouse, one which meant he didn't have to walk through water to reach the ale houses. He ran to the seafront to meet with Bill Mason and knew just where to find the leader of the press gang.

Tommy and Daniel played in the water until both were exhausted and then, with hands discretely touching, sat on the rocks waiting for the sun to do its work. They dressed in shirt and breeches then walked barefoot through the narrow lanes of the town. Daniel lived in Friery Street where Tommy waved goodbye, he broke into a trot along Hawk Street on his way to his home in Moons Lane but as he passed Old Tree Street half a dozen drunken ruffians barred his way. "You can come with us quietly or we can rough you up, what's it going to be?" Bill Mason sneered.

It took less than a second for Tommy's fists to start lashing out; two bleeding aggressors were on the floor in no time but a heavy bar across the back of his head sent poor Tommy to his knees before blacking out. Bill Mason slung his weapon over a wall and instructed his remaining men to put the unconscious boy into a sack. They carried him awkwardly passed his own house in Moons Street, to the dockside then up the walkway to the deck of a ship where he was dropped. Watching from the shadows of the setting sun, Matthew Quintal rubbed his hands with joy, it had cost him ten shillings but was worth every penny; Daniel Winterbottom would soon be his!

Chapter 2

TOMMY WAS WAKING UP aware of his unfamiliar surroundings; the floor was moving, the sound of creaking wood and ropes under strain, men shouting orders and then the ice cold water being thrown over him followed by laughter. "Get up you lazy cocksucker! You're not a passenger, you're here to work!"

Tommy was at sea, unsteadily he stood up supporting himself against the foremast; he turned a complete circle looking for land; there was none! "Why am I here, I should be at home with my mother and father!" He protested. More laughter from the crew; Tommy gawped at the ugly bunch of seafarers surrounding him until a more refined voice shouted louder than the rest.

"Leave him be and get aloft, the wind is increasing, give me more sail. The sooner we reach China the sooner I'll get you home to see your families again."

China was on the other side of the world, Tommy remembered from his schooldays. Sailors were at sea for years, some never returning, he thought while clinging to the mast as the ship pitched and rolled in the calm sea.

"Come with me!" The cultured voice took Tommy by surprise. At the rear of the wooden ship was a special cabin with the name, Captain Peter Harris, on the door. "Sit down and tell me about yourself, I have been told you are a carpenter."

Captain Harris was a little taller than the youth, just over six-foot, his narrow green eyes were like slits in his thin face, the crooked nose was his noble feature as was the way he spoke but it was his hands that caught Tommy's attention, they were huge, completely out of proportion to the rest of his body.

"Yes sir, my name is Thomas Fletcher; I'm just eighteen and finished my apprenticeship last week. Can you tell me how I arrived on this ship, sir?"

"I bought you from a bunch of scallywags who were going to sell you to the navy; You'll be much better looked after on the Lady Jane than any navy ship and I can always do with an extra pair of hands on a long journey," he stood away from his desk displaying an erection, Tommy's eyes went straight to the bulge. "This could be a very comfortable passage for someone as pretty as you."

The thought of escape was receding fast, with every minute that passed, the ship was further away from land and although a strong swimmer, Tommy was no fish. Should he bow to the captain's subtle suggestion or rebel, demanding his freedom?

"What would you like me to do for you, sir?"

"Get out of those wet rags and let me see what you look like!" The two garments were stuck to Tommy's body after having water thrown over him and the captain was getting impatient. He came towards Tommy and ripped the shirt from his back then with two hands on the waistband of his breeches pulled them apart as if they were made of paper. The naked boy stood with his hands by his sides while being scrutinised by the ship's master. Wandering hands ran through Tommy's dark curly hair, over his broad shoulders then across his powerful chest; Tommy closed his eyes as the fingers of one hand glanced over his stomach and into the small patch of hair. The other hand enclosed itself around the flaccid stem and then the balls were cupped. The captain stood back admiring the Adonis. "An all over sun tan on such a beautiful and muscular body. You are by far the best looking lad we've had on this ship for many a year. Make it hard!" His tone changed and Tommy quickly jerked his cock into motion bringing it passed his belly button in seconds, "oh, yes! I think you are just what I need for a successful journey." He opened a cupboard, "put these on, we can't have you walking around the ship like that, the crew will eat you!" He roared.

The young carpenter pulled on the very tight breeches made of some thin see-through material and a matching shirt, both garments would fit a small fourteen-year-old, he thought. The captain rang a bell and the door opened immediately, a man in his early twenties, clean shaven with bright blue eyes looked at Tommy and smiled.

"Find him somewhere to sleep and don't touch him; he belongs to me!"

It was dark when Tommy's father knocked on the door where Daniel lived; he was told the boys left Cockside where they had been swimming three hours ago. Both families, along with their neighbours, began searching the streets of Plymouth.

The hammock took some getting used to as did the rocking of the ship. The man who showed him to his swinging bed was called 'Horse', he never told Tommy why but it reminded him of his friend Daniel who, he feared, he would never see again.

The captain said he had been bought which meant somebody had sold him; Tommy racked his brains trying to remember anyone with a grievance who might have bad feelings against him; he could think of nobody! He was woken by water pouring over him and the noise of shouting, of the wind tearing through the sails and the rigging straining against the ship's sides. He fell from the hammock onto the sloping lower deck thinking the ship was sinking then clumsily sought his way up to the main deck to hear shouting voices calling to the heavens where sailors, high up in the masts, were wrapping the sails.

"You shouldn't be up here, young Fletcher; you could be a danger to yourself especially if you were to fall overboard!" Captain Harris warned.

"Are we sinking, sir?" Tommy asked fearing for his life.

"This is a mere strong wind, nothing to worry about; it will blow itself out by morning. Why don't you wait in my cabin, weather like this excites me!" In the darkness the captain grabbed Tommy's hand and held it against his crotch.

The carpenter bumped and fell but finally found his way to the back end of the dancing ship then waited in silence in the master's black room hanging on to anything that didn't move; his stomach heaving at every lurch of the bouncing vessel. "Take a few deep breaths," a soothing, mellow voice spoke quietly in the darkness, "It's me, Horse, don't be alarmed, I'm here to light some candles." The captain's servant used a spill to light the tapers throughout the cabin creating eerie shadows around the walls. "If you please the captain he will treat you well."

"What do I have to do?" Tommy asked naively.

"Suck his cock, lick his balls and wash his arse with your tongue!"

"I don't think I could do that!" Tommy's stomach was already on the verge of evacuating anything still inside him.

"Think again, Tommy, if you don't like that you'll be in the crows nest every night and it gets pretty cold up there, so cold your hand freezes to your cock while you're wanking."

Thankfully the wind eased and the ship began to settle; Tommy could stand unaided again. The door opened and the captain immediately removed his jacket and shirt; it was warm in the small room with so many candles burning. "Strip!" Just one word, an order, no, a command told Tommy to make his choice and as he hated the cold he took of his tight shirt and breeches. He was naked long before the captain and stood motionless waiting for instructions. "Don't just stand there, pull my boots off!"

Tommy watched the toes curl and stretch as each boot was taken off then he began massaging the liberated feet; pleasing the captain without licking his arse was uppermost in his mind.

"Help me with these pantaloons, Fletcher!" The young carpenter unbuttoned the garment and eased it over the biggest cock he'd ever seen; it reached more than half way down his thigh and it wasn't even hard! "Why don't you put some life into it?" Tommy's hand enclosed around the massive organ and slowly jerked it to and fro. "I can do that myself, but I can't suck it!"

The boy was on his knees with the foul smelling cock an inch from his face, he took a deep breath and placed his lips over the drooling crown and almost vomited. It tasted nothing like Daniel's; his friend's cock was always clean and smelled sweet from swimming every day.

He allowed his tongue to travel up and down the enormous length then cupped the captains huge ball sack with both hands, the carpenter heard the captain sigh then felt hands on either side of his head forcing his mouth to go further onto the endless column.

"Lick my balls!" The command was unambiguous, there was no way Tommy could do something else to please his master and it was getting closer to the worst thing he had been told to expect.

A knock on the door saw a foot push Tommy away and the captain cover himself with his jacket. "Yes?" He called angrily. Horse stuck his head in the doorway.

"The bos'on says some of the rigging needs replacing, sir. That storm tore some of the ropes away from the side . . ."

"It will have to wait until daybreak, I'm busy! Can't you see that?"

"Yes sir, sorry sir!" Horse closed the door and the captain moved from his chair to the bed. Even in the flickering candlelight Tommy could see the snow-white skin of the captain contrasting against his own healthy colour obtained from his weekend adventures with Daniel.

Captain Peter Harris's body was hairless, which pleased Tommy; if he closed his eyes and breathed through his mouth maybe, just maybe, he could imagine it was his lover. Tommy knelt beside the bed and placed his head between open thighs, his fingers tantalising the sensitive skin before his mouth made contact with the heavy sack. He nibbled on the wrinkled bag, something Daniel did to him, then very slowly licked around each ball in a soothing motion; Peter Harris closed his eyes and moaned at the relaxing pleasure the new boy was giving him, worth every penny he'd given to Bill Mason he thought as he drifted off to sleep.

Snoring alerted Tommy to gradually ease off, he covered his master with a sheet, picked up his two garments then snuffed out the candles before quietly making his exit. On the way down to his hammock he bumped into Horse. "That was quick, it normally lasts a couple of hours."

"The captain fell asleep, I covered him and left, did I do wrong?"

"No lad, this is going to be a long voyage, there'll be plenty of time for you to find out what he likes best."

Tommy remembered he was naked and with Horse's hand was on his shoulder squeezing gently his cock swelled, touching the man's thigh, "follow me," a hand grabbed Tommy's wrist and pulled him through dark passageways and down steep stairs until they could go no further; they had travelled the length of the ship! The carpenter leaned against the sloping keel and felt wet lips surround his limp flesh; it responded in an instant. The slurping tongue and groping hands reminded him of the storehouse; Tommy also recalled the sound he heard as he and Daniel were leaving their secret place. What if it wasn't as secret as they thought?

Horse's lips tightened their grip around the carpenter's stiffness, while at the same time a finger probed the hole, prompting the youth to gyrate his hips. Tommy could hear his companion jerking himself off getting faster by the second; another digit joined the first and it was too much for the boy, he moaned loudly and sent a fountain of fresh boy-cum down Horse's throat then felt warm juice splash over his legs.

"I'll take you back to your hammock," Horse whispered, "you'd never find it by yourself!"

Chapter 3

THE NIGHT WATCH CRAWLED into their hammocks as the rest of the crew got out of theirs. Tommy followed Horse to the mess where a bread-and-slops concoction called breakfast was eaten, then all assembled on deck to listen to the bos'on detail the workload. Chores included swabbing the deck, repairing the sails and fixing the damaged rigging. The new boy was given a mop and bucket and an area to clean. Tommy listened carefully at the sounds coming from the rigging high in the air, the crew were singing, "what are they singing, Horse?" Tommy asked the nearest of the crew.

Horse stepped closer and whispered, "Captain Pete beats his meat, he heats it up for you to eat!" Then put a finger to his mouth to indicate silence.

It was a warm evening when Matthew Quintal knocked at the house of Daniel Winterbottom. "Do you want to go somewhere with me!"

"No thanks, Matthew, I'm waiting for news of Tommy, he's been missing for a couple of days and I'm worried something has happened to him."

"He's probably run away to sea, I saw him down by the docks around this time yesterday."

"He wouldn't go without telling me first."

Matthew Quintal wasn't the brightest star in the sky and when he said, "he might, besides you said you wouldn't mind having my big cock up your arse, we can go to the storehouse and do it!" Daniel began putting two and two together.

"You were there yesterday, weren't you? You were spying on us!" Daniel pushed the older boy so hard he fell into the narrow street. "Tommy said he heard a noise, it was you! What have you done with my friend?"

Matthew began bawling, "you will never see him again, he's on a ship to China and if you don't believe me ask Bill Mason."

Daniel shut the door, he knew how Bill Mason made his money; he went to his tiny room and sat on his bed where he cried and cried until there were no more tears left.

It was late afternoon on the second day at sea when Tommy was summoned to the captain's cabin. Peter Harris was lying naked on top of his bed and beckoned the youth towards him. "When you enter my domain, you are here for one purpose and one purpose only, don't make me tell you to strip out of those clothes a second time!" he spoke with well-practiced authority.

"How can I please you today, sir?" Tommy was undressed.

"You can start by letting me taste yours, make it hard, always make it hard when you're close to me."

It wasn't a problem making it stiff, for Tommy always had a hard-on; ever since he reached puberty his cock had a mind of its own! The captain's lips greedily sucked on the column, gulping it into his throat. Fingernails dug into the soft flesh of the boy's bum cheeks while his hips swung to and fro. He felt the tide rising and couldn't hold back, but should he tell the captain or just let it happen? "I'm coming, sir." Tommy whispered, then poured his seed down Peter's throat.

"Now, do the same to me and if you make me come, I'll tell you who's idea it was to place you on the Lady Jane."

Tommy ignored the smell of stale piss and went straight down on the captain's enormous cock, sucking all the way down and back up twice every second, his fingers groping the officer's ball sack and probing beyond into the matted fur around his hole, He was eager to know the culprit's name so he could plan his revenge no matter how long it took. Tommy had three fingers of his left hand up the captain's arse, his mouth continued lathering the crown with saliva while his right hand wanked his master's cock. The boy knew something was about to happen when the captain's ball bag tightened and he began trembling. It was like the master was having a seizure, his whole body wobbled like a jelly, then the wave of warm thick milk shot into Tommy's mouth, he had to swallow quickly. If he thought about it he would probably vomit again.

Horse sat on a seat outside the captain's door. It was his duty to make sure nobody entered the cabin without first being announced but after last night's fun with Tommy, Horse was tired and had fallen asleep so when the bos'on needed extra hands to repair the sails he needed to ask the captain's permission first to get last night's crew from their hammocks.

The ageing seafarer couldn't believe his eyes when he saw his captain being serviced by the new boy, he'd heard rumours amongst the crew but put it down to gossip; now he'd seen it with his own eyes he was unsure what to do.

"Ahem! Excuse me captain but I need more hands on deck to repair the sails from last night's storm."

Captain Peter Harris hated being disturbed while fantasising with some beautiful boy and to say he was furious would have been an understatement. He pushed Tommy away from the bed exposing himself to the bos'on, who's eyes almost sprang from their sockets at the size of his master's massive pole. He yelled at the top of his voice, "fuck off out of my cabin and Horse get your arse in here!"

Horse had woken just as the bos'on entered but was unable to prevent him from catching the captain in the act. "Sorry sir, I fell asleep!"

"I'm going to give you something that will remind you of today for the rest of your life." The captain began dressing as did Tommy, he didn't dare ask for the guilty person's name.

Peter Harris was fuming, outraged that he had been caught, he dragged Horse onto the deck and called to the bos'on to strip the young man naked and tie him to the foremast. The captain went below while his orders were carried out but when he returned he was carrying a long whip. Tommy looked at the naked Horse and realised how he got the nickname, he really was built like a stallion! The captain was big but Horse had an extra couple of inches and was easily twice as wide. Tommy was shocked when he realised what was going to happen to the young man; with the exception of the steersman the crew were assembled to observe the cruel event. "Bos'on, you will carry out the punishment, ten lashes for falling asleep while on duty and let this be a warning to anyone who crosses the line with me!" He aimed his last words at the bos'on.

The long whip snaked around Horse's body and he let out a yell that curdled blood. Before he could beg for mercy the second struck across his back peeling the skin as if it were a tomato, rivulets of blood crept from the open gashes, another scream of pain as the third lash opened more flesh. Men turned away in horror; to them Horse was a good man who satisfied their needs while away from their wives.

"Stand still and watch! Any man who closes his eyes will receive a similar punishment."

Tommy counted to eight when Horse fell silent, at least he can't feel the pain anymore, he thought. The last two stokes of the vicious whip fell onto a corpse! The silence of the men was frightening, all hatred-filled eyes stared towards the captain but nobody moved except Tommy; he walked to the mast and began untying the handsome man and rested him slowly to the deck, he then ran his fingers through the dead man's hair before kissing him gently on the lips. Tommy had seen dead people before but this was the first murder he'd witnessed.

Peter Harris returned to his elaborate cabin before any of the crew noticed his erection, the unintentional execution had excited him and he'd come in his pantaloons. He peeled off the tight-fitting garment and rang the bell before remembering his servant wasn't at his post anymore. He would have to find a replacement.

Disquiet was brewing amongst the crew, they wanted blood; even the bos'on was troubled, he felt responsible for the dead man, if only he hadn't used the whip so hard, if only . . .

"Fletcher?" The stentorian voice from the back of the ship called for Tommy. He ran to the captain's cabin fearing he may feel the whip on his back if he took too long. He knocked on the door waiting for a response, "enter!"

"You called for me, sir?"

"You will take over from Horse, your duties include warning me of anyone wishing to enter my cabin. If someone tries to force their way in you will stop them, with your life if necessary. You will sit on the seat outside the door and if you fall asleep you know the consequences."

"Aye aye, captain." Tommy took up his position outside the door. He been sitting for a minute or two when the bell rang; Tommy entered.

"Get those clothes off, I want to feel your tongue around my cock."

"Will you tell me the name of the person who sold me to you, sir?" Tommy asked while stripping.

"His name was Quintal, Mr Matthew Quintal. You will have about eighteen months to dream up ways to get your own back but in the meantime put your lips around this."

Tommy went to work licking and sucking but his mind wasn't on the job, he was thinking how sad Daniel must be, they had never spent a day apart before . . .

"Get on with it, now do the same with my balls!"

The smell coming from between his arse cheeks was nauseating and he was sure he would vomit!

"Now you will clean my back passage with your tongue," the captain turned over on the bed, positioned himself on his knees and elbows and waited for the fantastic sensation to begin.

This was the one command the young carpenter was dreading! The closer his nose came to the foul stench the more he heaved. He began at the crack slowly edging his way lower to where the crust began then using his saliva, dribbled onto the matted hair turning the clinker into liquid.

"Poke your tongue inside the hole,"

Tommy complied and half an hour later the disgusting job was complete, without dressing he grabbed his two garments and raced up on deck bringing up the brown liquid over the side of the ship, he washed out his mouth with seawater vowing never to do it again no matter what the penalty!

Chapter 4

Months passed and Tommy learned everything about the ship, the crew and especially the captain. He was called on to perform more revolting things to please his master; Fortunately no more arse licking but regular cock and ball sucking and if he didn't please his master he felt those huge hands spanking his arse.

On two occasions the ship encountered severe storms, Cape Horn was the worst, three men lost to the sea and four badly injured.

The ship was approaching some islands in the South Pacific when the tragic end came for the Lady Jane. It was dawn and there was little warning; Tommy was in the crow's nest and alerted the steersman but too late, the huge swell some sixty feet high emerged from the darkness and struck broadside enveloping the ship, turning her upside down and flinging everyone into the tempestuous sea. Tommy took a deep breath and jumped from the top of the mast as the Lady Jane began to list, he was spinning underwater for several minutes before eventually surfacing, the single wave had moved on and the sea was calm again, he called for any of his shipmates but heard no response, most had been asleep.

He was alone in the vast ocean with only a piece of the foremast as company. He straddled the wide pole straining his eyes, searching for land. After many hours he was becoming weary, the blazing sun and his acute thirst was making him dizzy, then by chance a bird flew overhead, putting a cheer in his heart, he knew he was close to land, and moments later he thought his eyes were playing tricks on him; it was a ship! Tall sails billowing with the wind were heading straight for him. He stood precariously on the unstable mast and waved frantically at the vessel. If he could see them why couldn't they see him, he moaned in desperation as the ship turned, he followed it through squinting eyes; the strong sunlight reflecting off the water was making it difficult for him to see. Then he saw land, the current was pulling him towards an island and using his arms as paddles steered the mast onto the beach of white sand. Strange looking trees bearing even stranger looking fruits greeted him as he traipsed inland to the high ground in search of water. From the summit he caught sight of a clearing on the other side of the island and the ship he had seen earlier was about to drop anchor. He ran as fast as his legs would allow, racing down the hill through thick undergrowth, ripping his two garments to shreds, until he was close to the tall ship. He listened intently as the men spoke; they were English! The crew had rowed to shore in the ship's boat and were unloading empty barrels, they carried one each on their shoulders, taking them inland then returning with them full. They were collecting water, Tommy surmised. He followed at a safe distance and found the stream and then, when it was safe quenched his thirst. He needed to know where the ship was headed, for all he knew it could be one of the pirate ships the crew of the Lady Jane told stories about.

A youth about Tommy's age sauntered away from the others to take a piss, the carpenter whistled just loud enough to get the boy's attention; he looked up and Tommy approached smiling at him. "I'm Tommy Fletcher." He introduced himself.

"They call me Alf The Red; it's because of my hair. My real name is Alfred Turner," he smiled back, "I've not seen you before on the Carousel."

"That's because I was on the Lady Jane until a big wave took the ship and the crew to the bottom of the sea. Where is your ship heading for?"

"We're on our way back to Plymouth with our cargo of silk and spices." Alfred Turner had the most beautiful smile; it reminded Tommy of Daniel whom he'd not seen in over six months.

"Do you think your captain would let me come aboard?"

"Let's ask him!" He beamed.

Alfred Turner had joined the Carousel on its outward journey almost a year before, he'd yearned for the sea ever since he could walk. His father was the previous captain of the ship until he retired. The new master, John Swallow, took Alfred under his wing and treated the boy as his own.

"Excuse me captain," Alf began, "this is Tommy Fletcher, his ship sank and he wants to join the Carousel."

"What vessel were you on?" The young captain was curious and suspicious; the youth could have jumped ship!

"The Lady Jane, sir, she was hit by a massive wave and turned over, I was the only survivor."

"Who was the captain?"

"That would be Captain Peter Harris, sir."

"So, 'Pete the meat' is dead?" He saw Tommy grin, "what's funny?"

"The crew would sing a song about the captain, sir!"

"Yes, I remember, I served with him many years ago." He smiled, "of course you can join our ship, but not as a passenger, you'll work alongside Alfred. Show him the ropes young man."

"Aye, aye, captain!" The red-haired lad replied.

Captain John Swallow watched the almost naked pair of cherubs grab a barrel each and disappear into the dense forest. "If only I was their age again!" He mused.

The Carousel sailed after two days of replenishing water and fruits, the crew were rested and clean from their daily swim and the wind was in their favour.

Alf had slung his hammock in the cargo hold; he enjoyed the aroma of the spices and was away from the snoring, farting and often smelly sailors. It was no surprise when Tommy found himself berthed in the same part of the ship; he had taken a liking to his new friend from the moment he saw him relieving himself against a tree, his wonderful sense of humour, the permanent white tooth smile and his beautiful muscular body reminded him in many ways to his lover, Daniel.

Alf glanced across to Tommy, "Why are you looking so sad?"

"I left someone behind in Plymouth, someone I love very much; I just hope he's still waiting for me when I return." Tommy realised he'd said 'he' when probably Alfred Turner was expecting 'she'.

"Maybe I could take his place until we reach land!" Alfred Turner whispered while reaching with his hand to touch Tommy's.

They spilled from their hammocks simultaneously, wrapping their arms around each other in a tight embrace. Hands groped, touched and squeezed wherever there was flesh. Tommy pulled away and stared into the boy's smiling eyes and a tear ran down his cheek, "Thanks, Alf; you will never know how much this means to me."

"You're not the only one who's missing affection; I also left a friend behind when I joined this ship."

The red-haired youth clambered onto the bales of silk and Tommy climbed on top of him, he kissed the soft sweet lips while his hands searched inside Alf's breeches, the steel hard rod was wet as Tommy's fingers manipulated the crown encouraging more of the sap to escape from the peehole, Alf pulled the chord, loosening the garment and Tommy's hand liberated the expanding cock. The carpenter kissed the boy's neck, chest, stomach and finally the rock-hard silky-smooth cock, licking around the helmet and down the shaft; the body beneath him shuddered and moaned. Tommy's fingers explored the two small balls and the thin piece of skin between the bag and hole, this drove his friend into a frenzied state, his legs started twitching and his arms began flailing, nothing had ever excited him like this before! Tommy's middle finger was at the opening; it tickled and tantalised before entering the cave.

Alfred Turner was in paradise, the tongue and lips around his cock was the best sensation he had ever experienced until the finger probed his hole but when his spiky nipples were tweaked he lost control and without warning, spewed a gallon of come down Tommy's throat.

The carpenter slowly pulled his mouth from the base to the top of Alf's cock and holding it steady with one hand squeezed then licked anything left in the tube.

"That tickles!" He grabbed Tommy's head and at the same time brought his knees up to his chest. In an instant Tommy spat out some come into his hand, lathered his cock with it and pushed hard into the waiting hole. "Oh! What you doing Tommy? That hurts!"

"Relax, Alfie, you'll get used to it!" The narrow opening was the tightest he'd ever stuck his cock into and when the boy below clenched his cheeks Tommy almost came. "You can do it to me afterwards if you want to." He smiled down at the youth but in the darkness it was probably unseen. Tommy pumped gently, not wanting to damage the boy's inside. It was a long way to England and he anticipated this would be a regular pastime on the voyage.

Alfred began jerking himself off, the initial pain had turned into pleasure and he was taking delight in the new experience, he flexed his sphincter around the oscillating probe not realising it would make Tommy come, "oh my God," he yelled loud enough to wake half the ship's crew.

"Shush! The captain's cabin is above your head!" Alfred giggled.

Captain John Swallow was well aware of what his charge got up to while lying in his hammock at night, he could hear the boy panting while beating off but now there were two of them he'd love to watch them perform; an idea came into his head.

The crew were assembled on deck and Tommy was singled out by the bos'on, "captain's got a special job for you, Fletcher; report to his cabin."

The first thing to cross Tommy's mind was the arse licking he'd done for Captain Harris, but Captain Swallow wouldn't have known about that perhaps he just wants his cock sucked, that was a job he enjoyed as long as the cock was clean.

"Come in, Fletcher, are you settling in all right?"

"Yes, thank you, sir."

"As I love the aromatic perfume of the spices we're carrying I was wondering, as you're a carpenter, if you could make some holes in the floor so the fragrance would fill my cabin," his hands went through waving motions as if the smell had already penetrated inside his room, "I also think a little heat would release the bouquet allowing the pleasant fumes to rise; take several lanterns from the storeroom and fix them securely; it will be your responsibility to keep them lit at night."

Tommy carried out his work without question, boring holes was not an unusual task although the location was. He replaced the carpet and was about to leave, "don't forget to clean the mess below."

A strong breeze was blowing from the west, the ship was under full sail and the crew were content, Tommy knew this because they were singing shanties whilst pulling on the ropes. He was in the crow's nest, the first time since the demise of the Lady Jane; he kept his eyes peeled for other ships and whales, the huge monsters that could smash a ship to pieces with a flick of its tail or so he had been told! He had jerked off four times already; there was little else to do. He'd watch the stuff blow away in the wind only to be caught in one of the billowing sails. When he heard the bell ring he clambered down the rigging; it was time to eat. His eyes were alert for any sign of Alfie, he hadn't seen him since breakfast. Then he saw something strange, several of the crew, including the bos'on were standing against a large barrel, their bodies were pressed hard against it and they weren't making conversation. Some had their eyes closed while other's began panting, "there's a space round this side, son," one of the crew called to him while he watched the peculiar event. Out of curiosity he stood next to the sailor and noticed a hole just below waist height; it was then he realised they had their cocks on the inside of the barrel and although his own cock ached from beating off all day he still copied the crew and immediately felt soft fingers grasp his length; fingers he recognised from last night, they were Alfie's! Tommy shut his eyes and dreamed of Danny as lips circled his helmet, a tongue licked the underside of his crown and a hand moved up and down his shaft bringing him to an instant climax.

Tommy was eating his meal when he saw his new friend enter the mess, they ate together in silence until Tommy asked quietly, "why do you suck cocks from inside a barrel?"

"How did you know?" Alfie was quite casual with his reply.

"You sucked mine half an hour ago! You don't think I could forget those gentle hands and delicate lips after last night, do you?"

"I like sucking cocks and by doing so inside the barrel I don't have to see who they are."

The darkness descended as soon as the sun went down and John Swallow closed the log-book for the day. He extinguished the candles and rolled back the carpet exposing the recently drilled holes; there were eight of them, which meant wherever the lads were performing, he would be able to watch! He lay flat on the floor peering through the small openings but saw only darkness, perhaps he was too early.

Tommy explained to Alfie the work he had done for the captain then went to the storeroom to fetch some lanterns, "I'll be able to look into your eyes while I'm fucking you tonight."

"And I'll be able to see how big your cock is before you stick it up me!" Alfie laughed.

Tommy lit the candles, placing them close to the openings, while Alfie stripped out of his breeches; he climbed to his favoured spot on top of the bundles of silk waiting impatiently for his friend, "I'm ready, Tommy!"

The carpenter hung the last lantern above Alfie's head, "I want to watch your face when I do it to you." He spat into his hand, rubbed the wetness over his crown then moved forward against the red-headed boy who had his legs high in the air. Tommy pushed gently until he passed through the gate then continued until skin touched skin; Alfie's eyes were closed but he had a wide smile on his pretty face.

John Swallow saw the faint flickering beams from the lanterns penetrate his cabin floor, he peered through the holes until he found the pair just a couple of feet away and began jerking his cock, however it wasn't enough; he wanted to be part of their fun.

"Am I hurting you?" Tommy asked.

"No, it feels really nice; you can do it a bit harder if you want!"

The naked captain left his cabin, for him the darkness wasn't a problem; he could walk from stem to stern of his ship blindfolded. The hold was down a short flight of stairs and the glow from the candles could be seen long before he reached the two youths. The new boy was still shoving his iron hard cock into Turner; he advanced silently until he was inches away from the entertainers but he wasn't there to watch, he wanted to take part! He reached out with his left hand, touching the rounded cheeks of the carpenter, he smiled as the youth looked around without slowing his rhythm; the right hand joined the left in stroking soft, smooth flesh, gradually moving between the boy's legs. The middle finger of his left hand eased into the cave and was gripped firmly by the excited youth who came an instant later.

When Tommy saw the captain wanking himself he knew he wasn't in trouble for fucking the boy and actually enjoyed the finger penetrating his arse as he came, however, when the finger was replaced by a cock considerably bigger than had ever entered him before he was tempted to yell out in protest but instead bit his lip. His own cock was still hard even though he had come moments before and began pummelling the red-headed youth beneath him once again.

Alfie was on another island; paradise island! With his eyes still closed tightly he slowly wanked his cock up and down not wishing to come yet; he desired the wonderful pleasure to last all night. He had felt Tommy come deep inside him and then, after a moment's pause, the lunging long pole continued in and out of his arse once more.

John Swallow was comfortable standing still while Fletcher did all the work, the youth's bum cheeks were tightening on every thrust into Turner's arse then relaxing on the way out. The slow measured movement was bringing him to a climax but he could do it in the carpenter's hole whenever he wanted; it was the redhead he loved!

Tommy felt two strong hands pulling him slowly backwards until his cockhead slid from the moist opening, his place was taken over in a second by the captain, maintaining the same tempo as before.

"Oh! Tommy, that feels so good!" Alfie was unaware of the changeover; his eyes were still closed!

The captain was sweating profusely as he increased the rhythm, his arse swaying to and fro as he held the boy's legs high in the air. This was something he had dreamed of doing to the pretty youth since the first time he'd laid eyes on him four years earlier and he was determined to make it last as long as possible!

Tommy was somewhat surprised with the ferocity the captain was fucking the boy he was supposed to be taking care of but dismissed it as animal lust and not gentle lovemaking. He closed the gap between his hard cockhead and the captain's arse allowing the tip to press against the hole, then he was inside. The tables had turned; now it was Captain Swallow doing all the work!

Alfie's cock was lying stiff against his stomach; his fingers locked together behind his head and without touching himself sent a fountain of cum over his chest and face. The boy's smile increased until he opened his eyes and saw who had given him the thrill of his life, "captain?"

John Swallow had fulfilled his desire, it was better than he ever imagined and witnessing the boy come sent an extraordinary wave of passion from his brain to his cock. Never in his life had he ever come so much, stream after stream of his warm milk poured into young Turner as he lay on his back, but the boy had his eyes open and could see it wasn't Fletcher fucking him, his mind began working overtime, if the boy told his father on his return to Plymouth he could lose his job.

Tommy withdrew his spent cock from the captain's tight arse and stood back waiting for whatever reaction there would be from his new friend.

It was Alfie who broke the silence, "thank you, sir, I hope I satisfied you well!" he sat up, grasped the still rock-hard cock then slid down from the bales and began sucking on the nine-inch probe.

The captain grabbed each side of the boy's head forcing the whole length down his throat and came again! Alfie stood up and smiled, then wiped his mouth with the back of his hand. John Swallow pulled the two boys toward him, an arm around each of their shoulders, "there's no need to have candles burning anymore, we'll go to my cabin in future, it will be much more comfortable!"

Chapter 5

THE COAST OF ENGLAND appeared through the morning mist, "Plymouth is a couple of hours away, young Fletcher," the captain affectionately ran a hand through Tommy's curly brown hair, "will you be joining us for our next journey across the world?"

"I may have someone waiting for me, sir, but if they've found somebody else I would be happy to serve under you again." They both laughed.

The whole of the crew were on deck as the Carousel docked, calling and waving to wives and sweethearts not seen for over a year. A tear fell from Alfie's eye as he hugged his pal, "thanks for your friendship, I'll never forget you."

"You have a good friend in the captain, he'll look after you. Look me up next time you dock!" Tommy left the ship with more money in his pocket than he'd seen in his life and began his search of Daniel. He walked briskly to Firery Street and knocked on the door.

Daniel had cried himself to sleep every night since his lover disappeared, he'd lost interest in his work and when he looked at himself in the mirror he saw an old man. What was the point of living? He'd asked himself a thousand times. Every day he hoped the next knock on the door would be his beloved Tommy.

"Hello Daniel!" Tommy smiled and fell into the arms of the boy he never thought he'd see again. They sobbed while kissing, cuddled while whispering loving words then cursed Matthew Quintal for separating them. "I need to get my own back on that snake-in-the-grass. He not only took a year out of my life but kept me away from you. I could kill him and dump his body in the sea but that would be too easy; I want to make him suffer the same hardships and degrading situations that I had to endure."

"HMS Nymphas is docking tonight to pick up supplies and will be leaving on the tide before dawn; the captain has a reputation for harsh punishment for those not toeing the line. I'll get Matthew drunk at the tavern then somehow we'll get him on the ship." It was agreed.

Matthew Quintal strolled into the Tavern and sat by himself in the corner as he did most nights; there was little else to do. He was a loner and had no friends so when Daniel sat close by and offered to buy him a drink he became suspicious. The last time they had spoken was when Daniel had thrown him into the street. "Why would you want to buy me a drink after what I did?" He slurred.

"I need someone to do to me what Tommy did, I not only miss him, I long for his cock up my arse." Daniel was convinced he'd take the bait. After they'd been drinking for a couple of hours the sailors from the king's navy began pouring into the tavern; HMS Nymphas had docked.

Tommy was getting fidgety, what would happen if Daniel became drunk before his adversary? What if the sailors started a fight? Eventually they emerged from the crowded drinking house; both looked ready to collapse! Daniel beckoned Tommy from the shadows and between them dragged the semiconscious Matthew Quintal to the gangway where the duty officer barred their way. "He's one of your men." Tommy smiled, "he asked us to see him back to his ship if he got drunk."

The officer stood to one side as the two youths hauled their prey onto the ship's deck leaning him against the mast.

Tommy had finally exacted retribution on the person who had dared to come between him and his lover.

Matthew Quintal ended up on HMS Bounty under the strict rule of Captain Bligh and was given 24 lashes for insubordination. He was one of the mutineers and died at the hands of his accomplices on Pitcairn Island.

The End

WAGON TRAIN LOVERS

Chapter 1

"IF YOU DON'T GET your team together, I'm leaving you behind." The grumpy wagon master yelled for everyone to hear.

"You said we'd be leaving at sunrise but it's still dark." Jack protested.

"Everyone else is ready, why aren't you?" Seth Brown was a miserable bastard at the best of times; it wasn't a good idea to upset him, especially in the morning!

Jack fixed the reins to the second of two oxen then mounted the wagon, he flicked the leather strap urging the animals into motion and the wheels began to turn; his was the last to leave.

Jack was just eighteen-years-old, almost six-feet tall and had a strong muscular body, his handsome boyish face radiated beauty while sparkling, white teeth and short, brown curly hair only emphasised his good looks. With dark skin from toiling farmland since he could walk, Jack was a picture of health.

He began his adventurous journey from his homestead near Springfield joining up with several families at St Louis to make the perilous trek to the west coast.

It was dawn and chilly, he rubbed his hands against each other the keep warm, the first rays of sun shone onto the hillside in front of him, but he knew it would be a couple of hours before feeling any heat. The blue sky suggested anther hot day just like yesterday then freezing cold at night. His mind was wandering, he must keep the wagon ahead fifty yards away; if he narrowed the gap he'd be sucking in their dust!

Jack's parents had died from a flu epidemic last winter and he was on his own, a neighbour brought the farm at a knock down price and suggested Jack start a new life. With the money from the property, he invested in a wagon and team of oxen plus everything else he would need for the long haul.

"Wagons ho!" Was repeated down the line and the procession came to a stop.

"Water your beasts and get something to eat, we're on the move again in one hour!" Seth Brown called. This was the trail boss's fifth and final trek from one side of the country to the other, it was getting too dangerous; settlers were converging on Indian land causing animosity and tribes were obtaining rifles from unscrupulous traders; those same weapons would soon be used to kill the peace-loving pioneers looking for a new beginning.

Jack was hot and sweaty, the sun was directly overhead and he needed to cool down. There was a bend in the river a few hundred yards away where he couldn't be seen by the other travellers, he stripped out of his trousers and swam naked like he had back on the farm. The cool, clean water was refreshing as he lay floating on his back, but he wasn't alone!

"You're Jack, aren't you?" A lad about Jack's age was also swimming downstream. "Would you mind if I travelled with you? I've got three sisters and they are turning me crazy."

Jack gazed at the young smiling face and his heart almost stopped, he was looking at the most beautiful creature God had created. "Of course not, I could do with some company. It'll stop me talking to myself!"

The youth climbed from the water and sat on a rock; he too was naked. But Jack's cock had swollen at the sight of the adorable boy with short blond hair and he was going to have difficulty leaving the water without exposing himself. He couldn't move his eyes away from the muscular body and the loose thick cock hanging between those powerful thighs.

Billy Blane's family were in wagon number four, he was the only male offspring and his three sisters, all senior to him, had controlled his earlier life by dressing him up in their cast-offs and as he grew into his teens felt unsure whether he was a boy or girl. His dominant mother and weak willed father meant he had no say in family affairs and had been planning to make his move away from them at the first opportunity. His heart had missed a beat when he had seen Jack join the back of the line a few days earlier. He watched him walk beside his wagon stripped to the waist and followed him whenever he took a piss . . .

In the distance they heard the wagon master calling time to move on; Jack had no alternative but to reveal his seven inches of hardness pointing to the sky. "I don't know your name, what do they call you?" Jack asked the lad who was licking his lips while watching the bouncing cock.

"My name's William, but most people call me Billy, that's a nice cock you've got, Jack!"

"It's been hand reared." He laughed.

They dressed quickly and raced back to the wagon where Jack steered his team in line with the rest of the train. The pair walked beside the animals for the rest of the day talking about anything and everything. Jack liked his new friend, he made him laugh; something he hadn't done much of since the death of his parents.

As the sun fell lower from the sky the wagon master found a clearing big enough to accommodate the fifteen wagons. They formed a circle, as a precaution, Seth Brown warned, in case there were hostile Indians in the area.

Jack and Billy stood guard, armed with rifles, until midnight when they were relieved. It was bitterly cold with the wind coming from the north and Jack jumped into the back of his wagon. "Can I get in with you? We could keep each other warm!" Billy suggested.

"Of course you can. I hope I don't snore, though!"

"You didn't last night!"

"How do you know?"

"I slept under your wagon."

There was barely room for one on the floor of the wagon with so many supplies on board and heads were almost touching when they laid down together. With arms wrapped around each other to keep the chill air away from their bodies Jack's cock began to respond to the closeness of the sweet-smelling boy in his arms. Suddenly a hand pressed against his hardness; his first thoughts were to push it away but it felt good, perhaps if he pretended to be asleep they wouldn't speak of it in the morning.

The buttons were being undone on Jack's trousers, fingers groped inside and touched his flesh causing it to strain and expand further than it had ever done before. "Oh, Billy, that feels so good."

"I wanted to do this at the river earlier today, but I thought you might not like it," Billy whispered in the darkness. He slowly began moving the smooth skin to and fro generating a tremor throughout Jack's body. "I think we're rocking the wagon," Billy giggled quietly.

Jack fumbled with the tight cord around his new friend's waist then plunged his hand inside the coarse material until he located the iron-hard staff. He heard a long sigh of pleasure as he thumbed the damp crown. The discomfort of the restricted space and hardness of the floor was compensated by manipulating hands. Jack couldn't believe someone could bestow so much enjoyment by touching him down there.

They were breathing hard over each other, Jack began moaning very quietly remembering how sounds travel further at night. "I'm going to spill, Billy!" He whispered then convulsed several times as his cock spewed the biggest load ever.

Jack felt lips touch his just as his hand was filled with warm liquid; Billy had also experienced his best orgasm with another person.

Chapter 2

The wagon master was banging on the side "prepare to move," it was dark and cold outside but when Jack felt the body next to him stir he found a new reason to feel happy and content with his life.

He kissed the boy's cheek, "come on, help me with the team." Billy jumped from the wagon and began hitching up the oxen; they were ready to leave!

Jack had a spring in his step and a smile on his face, having Billy by his side had given him a new confidence in himself and a reason for going forward. It was midday when the column came to an abrupt halt; there had been a landslide blocking the way to a steep hill with no other route to take. The leader removed his hat and scratched his head. Jack had seen the situation before after heavy rain on his parent's farm. He volunteered to chop some trees and use them as levers to toss the rocks over the side. "We'll give it a try but I doubt whether it'll work."

With axes taken from the jockey box, the two friends stripped to the waist and between them lopped two strong trees then, with the help of the men and some strong women, namely Billy's sisters, toppled the massive rocks into the ravine; the noise was like thunder echoing around the hills. A round of applause from grateful settlers took Jack and Billy by surprise. Each wagon had to be pushed to the top of the steep gradient then eased gently down the other side. This tiring work had to be carried out fifteen times; needless to say everyone was exhausted and Seth Brown made the decision to stay overnight as they were close to water for the animals.

As there was still an hour or so of daylight left Jack and Billy went to explore the countryside. The stream looked inviting and they swam and larked around until darkness fell. Jack dried using his shirt and while he had his eyes closed felt something touch his semi-hard cock; Billy was on his knees using his tongue, licking the pee-hole then under the crown. Jack's cock grew and grew, the foreskin pulled all the way back behind his helmet as Billy took the whole length in his mouth and began swaying to and fro. Jack reached for his friend's head slowing the rhythm before he spilled his seed again. The blond head continued with the slower motion, the lips clenching tightly around Jack's straining cock. A hand reached to his stomach while a second went between his legs, fingers eased between his arse cheeks and probed his hole. "Billy, it's going to spill." He tried to pull out of the boy's mouth but Billy held onto Jack's arse forcing him deeper into his throat. "Where did you learn to do that, it was the most fantastic thing to ever happen to me."

Billy washed his mouth in the stream, "my cousin Jake liked me to do it to him, he used to yell when the stuff came out."

"I would have as well but didn't want to wake any sleeping Indians!" They laughed.

The camp was quiet, everyone was sleeping except the guard who didn't even see them climb into the back of their wagon.

"Can I do it to you?" Jack asked as they snuggled beneath the blanket.

"Nobody's done it to me before!"

Jack pulled down the blond boy's trousers and allowed his tongue to locate the rising stem in the darkness. The clean smell of Billy reached Jack's nostrils sending a thrill of excitement through his entire body, then clumsily tried licking the moving pole. He steadied it with his hand moving the flesh up and down while placing his lips firmly around the crown; Billy moaned and began to shudder. Jack's free hand felt for the boy's stomach and small patch of silky-soft hair while his mouth descended lower onto the long, thick cock. The hand supporting Billy's cock traced a line under his small balls and found the warm space between his arse cheeks; a finger teased around the hole before entering and without a sound Billy flooded Jack's throat.

The noise of Jack gagging, coughing and spluttering must have woken everyone in Nebraska; it certainly alerted the guard and wagon master.

"What the hell's the matter with you making all this damn noise? You'll have every Indian in the country searching for us!" Jack couldn't speak, he still had a mouthful of juice and wasn't sure what to do with it; he began swallowing then wiped his face on the blanket.

"You should have warned me that would happen!"

"I'm really sorry Jack. It done it so quick I didn't know I was going to do it, honest." Billy apologised, "does that mean you won't do it to me anymore?"

"Well, not until everyone's gone back to sleep!" They both giggled.

Chapter 3

MORNING CAME TOO QUICKLY but Jack and Billy were up and ready to leave. Being the last in line had its advantages, nobody could see what they were getting up to; like taking turns walking behind the wagon completely naked to get an all over sun tan, or jacking off to see how far the stuff would go. The two youths had found a special relationship; they made each other laugh on long days of the same boring scenery.

A crunching noise resounded around the hills and the convoy came to a halt; Jack climbed up on his wagon to get a better view.

"What's happened?" Billy asked.

"It looks like someone's lost a wheel."

Billy pulled on his trousers and the pair raced along the narrow trail to see if they could help. It was the lead wagon and had to be repaired with some urgency, "it's going to rain and this low lying area is likely to turn into a river!" Seth Brown warned. Everyone began unloading the disabled cart, to lift it fully laden would almost certainly cause damage or a weakness somewhere else. A fire was hastily lit and the metal rim heated and restored to its original shape. Replacement spokes were fitted and in less than two hours the family were on the move again albeit minus several heavy items, the wagon master reckoned they were carrying too much weight. The first spots of rain began to fall and the caravan of wagons needed to reach higher ground before the soil underfoot turned to mud. Jack suddenly regretted being last in the queue; if there was another incident he could lose everything.

Billy saw the worried look on his friend's face and squeezed his hand, "thanks, Billy, I don't know what I would have done if you hadn't found me."

"You'd still be jacking off every night by yourself!" He laughed.

The gradient was steep and the animals were having difficulty climbing to the top, willing hands pushed hard to get the remaining wagon over the ridge as the narrow track below filled with water. Jack was in tears as he thanked everyone for saving all he owned. The wagon master decided to remain where they were until the weather improved, "we've had enough excitement for one day!" He declared.

The two youths stripped out of their wet clothes under the bonnet, although raining hard the air was warm, coming up from the south and they dried in minutes. Jack looked deep into the smiling eyes of his friend, "why do I get a funny feeling in my stomach every time I look at you? Why do I want to hold you in my arms whenever you're close? What do you think it is?"

"I've felt the same way since the day you joined the train, even before we spoke down by the river and that was no accidental meeting, I'd followed you hoping to get to know you, but in my wildest dreams I never thought we'd fall in love."

"So that's what's wrong with me; I'm in love!" Jack's smile widened as he flung his arms around Billy's muscular chest, "kiss me and tell me if I'm doing it right!"

"You're asking an amateur, I've had nobody to kiss before either." Their lips touched, gently at first and then hard, hands gripped, pinched and squeezed as they rolled around inside the wagon.

Seth Brown called time to move on but when Jack tried to hitch up the oxen noticed the yoke had separated from the shaft. "You go on, I don't want to hold you up," he told the concerned settlers in front, "it won't take long to fix it." Jack said confidently. Billy assisted in removing the broken pin but when Jack searched through the jockey box there was no spare.

"What are we going to do?" Billy was worried.

"We'll have to make a new one, we've the wood and the tools." They stripped under the hot sun and between them sawed, filed and shaped the pin until it fitted then reloaded the wagon and hitched the beasts.

The docile animals began pulling their heavy load along the level trail, Jack was annoyed with himself, he should have checked everything was ok when they stopped; why couldn't he have waited until darkness to have his moment of passion with his boyfriend, he laughed out loud and Billy glanced back. "You're my boyfriend!" He called and they both laughed.

The ground was drying fast and the warm southerly wind began turning everything to dust again, Jack climbed aboard his wagon for a better view, they were still heading west but the sun was getting lower in the sky.

"I think we should stop here and wait until morning; we could slide into a gully and lose everything." Jack unhitched the oxen again and checked the repair, while Billy prepared a meal. The warm southerly breeze continued into the night; they kissed, fondled and loved, "what else did you have to do to please your cousin Jake?" Jack whispered.

"He used to fuck me!"

"Did it hurt?"

"At first it did, after a while I got used to it."

"But did you enjoy it?"

"Not with him but I would with you." Billy laid on his back with the soles of his feet pointing to the stars.

The only thing Jack had fucked before was his right hand and he jumped at the chance of learning something new. He pressed his crown against Billy's opening and eased very slowly forward, his friend moaned as the tight gate opened allowing the intruder inside, "Jesus, Billy, this is wonderful, am I hurting you?" Jack could see the pained expression on his lover's face in the moonlight.

"No, Jack, you're being so gentle with me, you can do it all night if you want!"

Jack's balls swung against Billy's skin as the in and out motion increased in speed, "do I spill inside you or take it out?"

"You can do it inside me if you want; I love you, Jack!" Those few words made Jack climax; he emptied his cock into his blond friend. Billy moaned loudly as he jerked himself off while Jack was still inside him then smiled up at the muscular frame, "I really do love you, Jack."

"And I love you, Billy."

They covered themselves with a blanket and slept.

Chapter 4

A SOUND LIKE THUNDER woke Jack; it was still dark. He untangled Billy's limbs from around his body and took a piss. The first signs of dawn could be seen in the east; it was time to hitch up.

After two hours into daylight they began to increase their pace; they needed to catch up with the rest of the train or they would be lost. Jack climbed onto the wagon for a better view, "there's a cloud of dust a mile or so away, it could be them!" Jack was excited as he jumped down but Billy seemed apprehensive.

"I don't think that's dust, I think it's smoke!" Billy was concerned; although he didn't get on well with his kin they were, after all, still family.

"Maybe another wheel has broken, they were well overloaded before," Jack tried to sound casual but he too was anxious, "the wagon master said to burn anything they couldn't carry, remember?"

The track began a downhill slant and they were making good speed, every turn brought them closer to Billy's worst nightmare; he feared, as did Jack, that everyone had been massacred by the wild barbarians. The stories Billy had heard sent a shiver down his spine; he began to cry at the thought of his family being scalped!

Jack halted his beasts of burden a few hundred yards from the smoking wagon, although concealed by some trees, anyone on high ground could have seen him approaching. He and Billy pulled on their trousers, grabbed their rifles then advanced towards the encampment. The sound of people in pain reached their ears as they progressed carefully into the circle of wagons.

Pa, mom?" Billy called with a trembling voice.

Jack found Seth Brown with an arrow through his shoulder; several other men close to him were either dead or wounded.

"Pull that fucking thing out of me," demanded the leader.

Jack obliged. The arrow had passed through the wagon master's flesh and out the other side.

"Where are my family?" Billy was frantic with worry.

"The Indians took all the women and children, they always do that then they'll come back for the wagons and animals, they probably think we're all dead, but we'll be waiting for them." The leader was adamant as he struggled to his feet.

A dozen or so survivors were walking around in a daze; most families had never encountered violence or even aggression before and to be attacked so savagely was against their Christian upbringing.

Billy found his pa wandering amongst the slain Indians putting a bullet from his rifle into each one, making sure they were dead. The youth couldn't believe his eyes, his father was the most docile of men and wouldn't say 'boo to a goose' but there he was firing point blank into the redskin's heads shattering blood and brains all over the ground.

"Pa?" Billy touched his father's shoulder.

"They took your mother and the girls," he said as if in a trance.

"Me and Jack will get them back!"

Jack and Billy approached the wounded wagon master, "which way did the Indians go?" Jack asked.

"Over that hill." He pointed with his good arm.

Jack shoved his hand into a grease bucket at the back of the nearest wagon, it contained a mixture of animal fat and tar, "put some of this on your face and hair, Billy; today you and me are Indians." They jumped onto two saddled horses and with rifles in hand galloped up the hill in pursuit of the primitive murderers. They followed the tracks of unshod horses in the soft ground for about five miles then saw smoke from camp fires. Jack indicated to Billy to dismount; they were in woodland a few hundred yards from some tepees. A stream ran beside the encampment and that seemed the only way to get close enough to get inside and free the captives without getting caught. They left their rifles; they probably wouldn't fire if they were wet!

The two boys waded into the water then swam until they were within a few yards of the first tepee; a lot of activity followed as a score of almost naked horsemen covered in war paint headed back towards the wagon master's enclave. Jack pointed towards what looked like an animal pen; several people, huddled together, were guarded by two elderly Indians holding tomahawks, "wait here, I don't want any harm to come to you; I love you, Billy."

Jack crept from the stream advancing towards the enclosure; his dark skin and blackened face blended in perfectly, from a distance he looked like an Indian. He put a finger to his mouth to indicate silence from the prisoners. The two old Indians stood close to each other in conversation, Jack crept up behind them and slammed both heads together; a sickening hollow sound was followed by the two sentries crumpling slowly to the ground. Billy raced forward, found his mother and sisters and after a brief hug led them back to the stream. Jack picked up the hatchets then escorted the remaining women and children the same way ending up in the woods where the youths had left their horses.

The liberated but frightened captives had walked some four miles before hearing gunfire; the fight was still going on at the wagon camp. Jack and Billy peered over the hill, only four of the Indians were still alive, riding on horseback around the encircled wagons screaming and firing arrows at the remaining pioneers.

Jack grabbed Billy's arm, "come on; let's see if we can bag a couple each!" They jumped onto their steeds and charged down the hill with rifles in hand. Jack fired first and watched the Indian fall; Billy's shot also found its target. The two remaining redskins turned their attention to the two boys; Jack ducked as an arrow narrowly missed his head just as he fired his rifle. The warrior fell to the ground along with the last one; Billy had scored a bulls eye right between the eyes. A cheer rang out from the survivors as Billy and Jack rode into camp. The wagon master had been hit with a second arrow; this one was in his leg. Billy found his tearful father still alive and pointed to the freed women and children walking down the hill.

It had been a traumatic experience for everyone but now wasn't the time for celebration, it was time for burials. Four men, all husbands and fathers, had been slaughtered. It could have been more had the majority of men not been collecting water from the nearby stream when the attack took place. Holes were hastily dug and the bodies covered.

Seth warned of possible reprisals, "we've wiped out one renegade tribe of Indians but once word gets around there will be a lot more after our blood. Get your things together; we'll be moving on in ten minutes and you two watch your backs." He said to the two youths. They soon became paranoid, looking behind every few paces and even walking backwards!

It was well into the afternoon when the wagon train continued its journey it seemed to be moving more quickly than normal, fear has a habit of making people do things at a faster pace!

As darkness fell another circle was formed, no fires or lights were allowed, the sentries were doubled and everyone was told to sleep with one eye open. Jack and Billy had the four-to-six shift which meant no sleep after four in the morning. "Perhaps we should have an early night." Jack whispered. They climbed into the back of their wagon, "keep this beside you, just in case!" He handed Billy one of the tomahawks he'd taken from the raid. "Use it if you have to."

"I'd prefer if your cock went up there instead!" They both giggled quietly. The warmth of Jack's naked body against his soon had Billy aroused, he turned his back to Jack then reached around feeling for the hardness. He held the iron pole against his passage and eased back as his friend pushed forward. Jack reached under Billy's narrow waist and wrapped his fist around the bone hard cock moving it slowly to and fro; they were locked together in wild passion, masking the terrible events of the day. Jack pushed hard, his hips banging against Billy's arse cheeks, the rhythm was shaking the wagon, hanging items swayed and touched, tinkling like little bells. Billy began laughing, his body trembling in Jack's grasp; on the other hand Jack was oblivious to the sound, lost in the wonderful feeling of sex, the sensation of his cock sliding in and out of the velvet tube was the most thrilling thing in the world and nothing was going to distract him from his moment of pleasure.

When Billy jerked himself off in the past it was all over in a couple of minutes but Jack was more methodical; he squeezed, tickled, tantalised the crown with his thumb and found a thousand and one other ways to please the boy who was giving him so much satisfaction.

The problem arose when they 'spilled,' whoever came first prompted the other to do the same and it caused a ruckus of clattering instruments and utensils as the 'stuff' left their squirming bodies.

"Keep the noise down in there!" An angry voice called. They sniggered again; they were young and they were in love.

Chapter 5

"COME ON YOU TWO, it's your turn on guard!" The voice whispered. Jack jumped down and pulled on his trousers and shirt, picked up his rifle and box of ammunition then began patrolling the encampment; moments later Billy joined him. It was spooky, not a sound broke the silence in the complete blackness. It was warm, Jack had never known heat at night like this, the trees began to sway gently as a breeze sprung up and within five minutes it had turned into a howling gale. Jack and Billy had difficulty standing and raced back to their wagon; they grabbed ropes from the jockey box and tethered their wagon to the nearest tree then helped others do the same. One wagon was blown over before it could be lashed down, its contents spread over a wide area. There was no need to be quiet anymore voices were shouting at each other over the din of the storm. Jack tended to his spooked animals, stroking their heads to calm them down, they had served him well; he didn't want them to flee out of fear!

By sunrise the damage could be assessed, one wagon completely destroyed as if made of matchwood, the bonnets ripped off two others. Seth Brown, still in agony from his wounds, was at his wits end. He'd never come under attack by Indians before and never been hit by a sudden squall either. He gazed at the demoralised faces staring at him, they looked to him as their guide and leader; he felt it his duty to give them the option of whether to continue their journey or not. "We'll take a vote; those of you who want to go back to Independence raise your hands!" Nobody did. "Then let's get ourselves organised, we should be able to repair the bonnets if someone can climb the trees to retrieve them. Salvage what we can from the busted wagon and share its contents amongst the rest of you until we reach Oregon. Come on then, we haven't got all day." Jack and Billy helped the new widows pack up their belonging and it was midday before the wagon train was on the move again.

Billy walked behind the wagon, removed his trousers and danced naked under the warm rays of the sun, "you'll be mistaken for an Indian; you're almost black!" Jack predicted. The beautiful boy had changed colour considerably over the last few days, his muscles were more prominent and his patch of blond hair around his cock could hardly be seen. He still radiated a halo of gorgeousness that probably only Jack could see and had he met Billy in Springfield he would never have started this journey. In one respect it felt good being in love, but it now meant he was responsible for the welfare of his lover, if anything were to happen to Billy he would surely die himself.

"It's my turn to guide the animals," Billy began. "Let the sun caress your body."

"You're in a good mood today."

"That's 'cause I'm in love, Jack, and I'm in love with you." He kissed Jack on the cheek.

"Don't do that when Seth's around, he might get jealous." They both laughed.

Billy watched Jack from a distance, he worshiped his new friend and to see him walking behind the wagon naked caused him to get a hard-on. He loosened the cord supporting his trousers and began jerking off, "you'll go blind if you keep doing that!" Jack reminded him.

"It's not my fault if you're so good looking!"

Seth knew this area well, he'd stopped overnight in the same place for the past four years; a safe haven, perfect for shelter and fresh water. The Indians had always been friendly in the past, trading furs for tools but nothing could be taken for granted anymore and precautions were called for.

Jack's wagon completed the circle and while he tended the animals Billy began preparing a meal for them both. They gazed into each other's eyes as they ate the same boring food as yesterday and the day before, no words were spoken, it wasn't necessary; they were in love.

They took the dirty tins to the stream to be cleaned. "I'm going for a swim to wash that grease out of my hair!" Billy announced while dropping his trousers.

"Don't go too far out it looks like there's a strong current." Jack advised. He continued scraping the mess from the plates but when he looked up Billy was nowhere to be seen. He stood up and saw waving arms almost on the opposite bank, Billy was in trouble!

Jack swiftly pulled off his trousers and dived from the bank swimming as fast as he could but he too was soon caught in the fast flowing stretch and was being dragged downstream. He reached the far side swimming with the flow, searching for his lover. Around the next bend he saw movement in the water, there were three figures and one of them had blond hair, it was definitely Billy! Jack swam closer as the two dark skinned youths plucked Billy from the water, they were Indians and had also been swimming naked but with their local knowledge knew where it was safe. Jack climbed from the fast flowing stream, concealing himself amongst the rocks and bushes. The warriors hadn't become violent yet but may if they thought they were being threatened.

The taller of the Indians was fascinated by the blond hair, while the other began touching Billy's cock, pulling the skin back behind the crown.

Half drowned and lying on his back Billy Blane coughed up water from his lungs and as he slowly opened his eyes he glanced up to his rescuers. They were Indians! He jumped to his feet and shielded his cock with his hands, not because he was shy but because it had become hard.

The taller of the two braves had a stocky build and looked to be about Billy's age, he seemed fascinated by the almost white hair; the younger and smaller one appeared more interested in the paleface's cock. Young Billy was terrified, they may scalp him or lop off his cock with one of the tomahawks lying with their loincloths; should he put up a fight and try to escape? He weighed up the situation and began to calm his shaking body, they were not being aggressive towards him, in fact he found the caressing fingers running through his hair soothing.

The small Indian first touched Billy's stomach and then the top of the pink cockhead poking from finger-locked hands, he stared into the blond boy's light blue eyes, then, as they smiled at each other Billy relaxed, dropping his hands to his sides and allowing the boy to handle his hard pole.

Jack was only a few feet away waiting for his opportunity to rescue his lover but when he saw Billy smile at the pretty boy he became less tense and began running his fist up and down his own rigid cock.

The taller brave ran a pair of hands over Billy's shoulders, down to the small waist and over the soft firm cheeks of his arse, neither of the warriors had spoken with their mouths but seemed to communicate with their eyes.

Billy felt the head of a cock between his legs without seeing it, which was just as well; the enormous size of the pole almost made Jack call out to warn his friend but thought it better to remain silent and jerked off faster instead!

The blond boy took hold of the young Indian's long thin cock and watched the expression on the cute face just inches away change from a timid smile to ecstasy.

Big hands gripped Billy's narrow waist as the huge crown forced its way through an opening half its size; he drew in a massive intake of air, stood on tiptoe and arched his back towards the sighing Indian as the endless probe slowly entered him. But not a sound passed his lips; he was still unsure how they would react if he protested.

Jack spilled his seed for the second time, the thrill of watching was almost as good as taking part especially when he saw that strapping, muscular brave with the monster cock drive it up Billy's arse!

The younger Indian sank to his knees and started licking Billy's drooling peehole, then the whole cockhead disappeared into the boy's mouth until his nose buried itself in a small patch of blond hair. The grip on Billy's waist tightened and the thrusting cock moved faster inside him, what started as pain had turned into pleasure but moments later he felt the squirting fluid pulsating inside his passage. It was all over for the big Indian brave but not for Billy; the experienced tongue was giving him pleasure he didn't know existed, he pulled in his stomach as gentle fingers cupped his small balls, took in another huge lungful of air and spewed his stuff into the boy's throat. The lad looked up while Billy's meat was still in his mouth and winked, he hadn't finished jerking himself off. Billy felt the warm milk hit his thighs several times before he was allowed to have his cock back! The big Indian placed his arms around the other two and kissed Billy on the cheek; the younger one copied. Then the tall brave indicated with is hands the trail back to the wagon train without going into the water. Billy returned their kisses and with smiling faces the braves collected their belongings and walked in the opposite direction.

Jack waited until they were out of hearing range and whistled to his lover who turned, with hands on hips and a big smile across his face. "You'd never guess what just happened to me." He began.

"Let me think, I know, you got fucked by a couple of Indians!" Jack laughed, "I stood only a couple of feet away watching, I thought that big fellow was going to split you in half, you didn't see the size of his cock when it was hard."

"Why didn't you come to my rescue when they forced themselves on me?"

"Because you were enjoying yourself and besides that little guy was quite cute, I should have made myself known earlier."

"Hey, I thought you loved me!"

The water was calm in this part of the stream and was easy to cross; they walked along the riverbank as suggested by the friendly Indians to where Jack had left their dishes and trousers. It was dark as they walked into the enclave, a few of the pioneers were still awake chatting but most had taken to their beds. Jack and Billy climbed into the back of their wagon and snuggled together. "You really enjoyed that bone up your arse, didn't you?" Jack whispered

Billy giggled out loud, "I've never heard it called a bone before." He reached down and grasped Jack's permanently hard cock and moved it to and fro; all Jack could see in his mind was the muscular Indian fucking Billy's arse down by the rocks. It only took a few moments to drench his lover's hand in warm liquid. "Wake up you two, you're on Indian watch!" A voice called from outside.

Jack laughed.

Chapter 6

JACK COULDN'T GET THE memories from yesterday out of his mind and kept glancing back to Billy who was walking on his hands behind the wagon. It was a gradual uphill slope and progress was very slow, although he'd cuddled his lover in his arms throughout the night he wanted to touch and fondle him again. "You'll get your balls sunburned walking like that!"

"You can cool them down with your tongue when we stop later. And I can show you what the cute Indian boy did to me with his mouth." Billy somersaulted, landing on his feet.

The sun was at is highest when Seth called a halt, he knew the best and easiest places on the trail for the pioneers to collect and water their animals.

Billy unhitched the oxen and led them into the water where they satisfied their thirst while Jack took a swim washing off the dust clinging to his sweaty body. It would be his turn to walk behind the wagon until dusk. He swam slowly from one side of the crystal clear stream to the other; his mind fixed on his pretty lover.

The blond boy re-harnessed the animals to the wagon then dived from the bank heading towards his friend; he swam underwater and grabbed hold of the pair of bollocks hanging low. Jack yelled thinking a water snake or big fish had attacked him. Billy giggled; it was what he did much of the time and another reason why Jack loved him so much.

The wagons moved along the smooth trail following a track made by hundreds before them. The flat ground beside the river made it easier for the animals as well as the humans on foot.

Naked Jack ran from the wagon a hundred yards or so then raced back, mainly to break the boredom but also to keep his body in good shape. Back in Springfield he was chopping trees, sawing logs and steering the plough, but walking didn't improve his strength. He enjoyed the uphill slopes when he could use his muscles pushing the wagons to the top.

"Save some energy for me, I might want you to stick your thing up me later."

"I don't think I'll touch the sides after what I saw go up there yesterday," he panted, "it'll be like fucking a bucket." They both laughed again.

Jack ran a lot further away from the wagon this time, it was getting late and would be his last run of the day. He was going at his maximum pace when he rounded the bend and came face to face with the same boys he'd seen at the stream with Billy. They were just as surprised to see him as he slid to a halt and the taller one reached for his tomahawk. Jack was unprepared for fighting, being naked left him at a disadvantage, besides he didn't want a scrap with these two fine specimens he wanted some fun. The younger, pretty boy couldn't take his eyes from Jack's cock which was growing by the second, he reached out a hand as the foreskin peeled back behind the crown, wrapping soft gentle fingers around the girth. The bigger youth touched Jack's muscled shoulders and arms, then his chest and stomach. The two Indians were on either side of him and their loincloths were pointing straight up. Jack felt under the leather, gripping a cock in each hand but then remembered Billy was still with the wagon and probably worried about him.

Using sign language he indicated for them to follow him, he ran at a slow pace until he could see his wagon; Billy was walking backwards searching for him.

Seth Brown had already come to a halt and was organising the circle in a wooded area and again close to water. Employing the same method, Jack told the Indians to wait a short distance away, they glanced at each other nervously but complied.

Billy was loosening the reins from the oxen and was more than a little distraught when Jack finally showed himself. "Where have you been? I almost died worrying about you!"

"I found your two friends from yesterday, they're waiting for you in the woods."

"Why didn't you say so before?" He beamed.

With the animals watered and bedded down for the night the two boys went in search of the Indians. There was about an hour of daylight left and a swim was suggested by Billy, he was covered in dust from following the preceding wagons all afternoon. The Indians were already splashing, ducking and diving in the river and recognised Billy immediately because of his hair, then saw Jack. The younger brave seemed to have taken a shine to the dark-haired muscleman, swimming up to him and planting a kiss on his cheek whereas the taller native grabbed hold of Billy trying to squeeze the life out of him.

Jack held the boy away from him, "Jack, I'm Jack," he pointed to himself.

"Jark?" The boy replied.

That's close enough, he thought, "You, what are you called?" He gestured towards the boy.

"Kurux," the boy hunched his shoulders imitating some sort of animal.

Jack picked up a white stone holding it against his head and pointed to his lover, "Billy, Billy," he repeated.

"Birry?"

Then Jack indicated to Kurux's powerfully built friend by flexing his muscles. The boy laughed, "Skirik."

Kurux cuddled up closely in the water and began pulling on Jack's cock, the boy's own long slim rod was pressing against Jack's thigh and in urgent need of release.

If somebody had told the youth from Springfield a couple of weeks ago that he would be having the time of his young life with a wild Indian boy he would never have believed them.

He took hold of the bone and gave Kurux what he desired. Jerking the loose foreskin to and fro, he watched the small body squirm under his skilled touch until it convulsed and spilled under the water. When the lad recovered they moved to shallow water where the boy knelt and took Jack's cock in his mouth. It felt like the kid had a thousand tongues as his head raced up and down on Jack's rod. He had to grip the sides of the Indian's head to slow him down.

Billy laid on a smooth rock, his legs on the shoulders of Skirik, every muscle in the Indian's strong body flexed as his massive cock shunted to and fro. Billy had seen its size but wasn't scared; it probably hadn't grown too much in the last twenty-four hours!

The blond boy jerked his own cock slowly at first but as he sensed the Indian was about to spill he increased his speed and they both yelled at the same time.

Jack revelled in the pleasure the lad was bestowing on him, he ran his fingers through the long black mane and over smooth shoulders and when he spilled it was the most that had ever spewed from his cock. He picked the boy up in his arms as if he weighed nothing, laid him on the grass and sucked the slender stiff bone. Kurux moaned loudly with closed eyes as Jack's lips enveloped the crown then moved gradually towards the base; while one hand explored the small chest and stomach the other fondled the tiny balls and searched for the opening. A finger penetrated and the Indian boy spilled into Jack's throat but the bone didn't soften, it remained hard. Jack was aware of the closeness of Billy and his Indian friend but he didn't stop until he'd satisfied Kurux again.

There were hugs and strange words spoken by the pair of dark skinned natives, Jack and Billy had made friends with so-called savages; but they had found the only thing wild about these two was their lust for sex.

Skirik and Kurux went to the cave they had made into a temporary home while the two pioneers walked back to camp in time to begin their look-out duty, it was ten o'clock and dark. Seth was smoking his pipe when Jack approached. "What are the Indians like around here?"

"They are Pawnees, we never have any trouble from them, they make good scouts and hunters, we'd never go hungry with a couple of those around. It's a pity we haven't met any, with my injuries we could have done with some help."

"I met a couple of friendly Indian lads earlier; I think they may be looking for a job."

"Well, if they're still around in the morning, send them to me and I'll have a word with them."

"You speak their language?"

"Of course, how else am I going to communicate with them?"

Jack raced to where Billy was jerking off for the hundredth time and told him the news. They hugged each other and jumped up and down with excitement.

An hour before dawn Jack and Billy followed the track back to the cave where the two Indians were cuddled together. At first they were startled at being woken from their dreams but with some expert sign language Jack persuaded them to follow him to the enclave.

"These are the two lads I told you about, Mr Brown." Jack began.

The wagon master held a brief conversation with them before saying, "they're your responsibility, Jack. The big one is called Grey Wolf and his younger brother is Bear. As the rest of the settlers might not take too kindly to seeing Indians roaming around the camp after the ruckus we had the other day, you and your pal Billy will look after them, you'll feed them and they will sleep in your wagon. Do you have a problem with that?"

"No Mr Brown, I think we'll all squeeze in together somehow!"

The End

THE TOURIST

Chapter 1

"FLIGHT MX 715 TO Tenerife is now boarding at gate 22." The voice announced. Brad picked up his flight bag and joined the long queues of restless holidaymakers waiting to board their plane; it had been delayed for over two hours!

Bradley Thompson had never flown before and was more than a little nervous; he'd led a somewhat sheltered life living with his grandparents since the death of his mother when he was nine; he never knew his father. A group of college pals had got together to holiday in the sun in January and the only place in Europe that could guarantee any warmth was the Canary Islands, an archipelago off the coast of Africa.

His fellow students had left a week earlier to begin their fortnight stay but Brad could only get a seven day break because of the part-time job he'd just started.

When his elderly neighbour heard he was going he offered to drive him to the airport and accompany him to the check-in desk, after that he would be on his own.

He had followed the people in front to the departure lounge and was copying again as he handed his boarding card to the smiling steward. He must have appeared totally lost as the same steward showed him personally to his seat and lifted his hand luggage, stowing it in the locker above his head.

Brad took interest in the safety film then braced himself for take-off; the Boeing 757 roared along the runway and into the sky. 'That wasn't so bad after all!' He muttered to himself at the same time releasing the huge lungful of air stored in his chest and relaxing his tight grip on the armrests. As the in-flight film had recently been shown on television he connected his Ipod then closed his eyes for the long journey. The sound of the seat belt light coming on woke him from his dreams; the plane was coming in to land, he'd slept for over four hours!

It was after ten o'clock when the tourists reached the arrivals hall; he grabbed his holdall from the carousel then searched the faces waiting to meet the passengers; he recognised nobody and the meeting point where he expected to find his friends was deserted. An hour passed and Brad was getting desperate, he didn't know the name of the hotel where his colleagues were staying so couldn't contact anyone.

"I'm driving back into town if you want a lift."

Brad was startled by the smiling man. "Thanks but I'm waiting for friends, they should have picked me up an hour ago."

"Well, you can't stay here all night, the police don't allow it. You're quite welcome to stay at my place and we can look for your friends in the morning."

"Thanks, I would appreciate that," the youth smiled, "my name's Brad, by the way," he held out his hand.

"I'm Mike, welcome to Tenerife." They shook hands.

Michael Young had lived on the sunshine island of Tenerife for many years and was a bit of a recluse. Living in a small farmhouse high up in the hills and isolated from any neighbours, he was a sun worshipper and spent most of his time tending the many plants in his garden. He'd had few interests other than his horticultural hobby but as soon as he'd seen the youth by himself at the airport, wild thoughts entered his head.

The pickup truck left the airport car park and began its climb. "What do you do back in rainy England?"

"I'm at college by day and stocking supermarket shelves in the evenings."

"Any hobbies?"

"Not really, I'm a bit of a bookworm, I like to read."

"Nothing wrong with that, education is a marvellous pastime, much better than playing games on a computer. Got a sweetheart waiting for you back home?"

"No, I've got nobody to go back to, I live with my grandparents and they're off to Australia in a couple days to see my aunt and uncle and won't be back until May."

The conversation went on for ages and Brad wondered if they were doing an island tour in the total darkness. Finally, a small building appeared in the beam from the pickup's headlights.

"You'll have to forgive the mess, I wasn't expecting company." Mike opened the door and switched on the dim light. "No mains electricity up here in the Gods, I'm afraid, you'll hear the generator kick in as the power goes down."

This was definitely not what Brad had expected; he'd paid for a four star hotel, not a hovel half way up a mountain, but it was warm inside and cosy. Many pictures and photographs hung on the walls, a couple of small armchairs, a dining table, two wooden chairs and a carpet on the floor more or less filled the area along with an assortment of ornaments and plants; the room was all shades of green with so much foliage. "Give me your bag, I'll put it in the bedroom there's more space there."

Brad followed his host; a double bed and wardrobe left little room for anything else and he wondered where the toilet might be, if one existed at all!

"The bathroom is through there," Mike pointed to a door and Brad reluctantly opened it fearing what disgusting odour might hit his nostrils. But he was pleasantly surprised; a four-piece pink suite with tiled floor and walls and all smelling of roses.

"Wow! This is more like it! Sorry, I didn't mean to say that. I shouldn't be ungrateful for you taking me in like this."

"Get yourself showered and freshen up while I get us something to eat, you'll find a clean towel on the back of the door."

The youth stripped out of his clothes and stepped into the shower; he was half expecting to be hit with a cold spray but to his delight the water was warm and the perfumed soap soon had Bradley Thompson singing.

Michael Young watched through the two-way mirror; the beautiful youth was washing his perfectly shaped young body and as he turned to face his reflection, his host gasped at the size of the cock swaying to and fro, this was without doubt his best specimen yet.

"There's a dressing gown for you to wear, I've put your clothes in the washing machine." Mike called through the open door.

Brad thought it a bit strange that someone would wash his clothes but put it down to being friendly. "Thanks." He called back and stepped from the shower, dried and wore the silky Japanese style gown.

"I hope you like Chinese food, I love it and have a freezer full of all sorts of things and the best part is, it only takes a few minutes in the microwave." Mike was also dressed in a similar gown.

By the time the meal and a bottle of wine was finished it was well after midnight, they washed the dishes between them in the tiny kitchen then Mike suggested it was time for bed, "I hope you don't mind sharing, I don't think I snore."

"I probably wouldn't hear you anyway, I'm so tired."

Mike watched Brad remove his single garment; taking in the view of white cheeks contrasting against last summer's faded tan, before switching off the light.

The youth laid on his back, he had always slept that way and when an arm rested on his stomach he thought it strange but never moved although when the hand on the end of the arm began moving into his pubic hair he thought it even stranger! Brad had not at any time had a sexual experience, he'd never been attracted to women or men for that matter, the situation had not occurred like the one he was in now.

Something was moving, his cock was growing by itself and fingers were touching it sending a weird but wonderful sensation through his body. He heard himself moan in the silence then the bed covers came off and Mike placed his mouth over Brad's crown and in an instant Bradley Thompson had his first orgasm. He convulsed as if having a seizure until the fountain stopped erupting.

Mike turned on the light and reached for a towel to wipe his mouth. "You've not done that before, have you?"

"No sir, that was the first time."

"You mean to tell me you have never had a wank?"

"No, never."

"Then if you're ready, we'll do it again." Mike left the low powered light on.

Brad remained lying on his back waiting for the mouth to cover his rock-hard cock again; the host was slow and easy, wanting to make it last a little longer the second time! The bulbous crown smelled of the perfumed soap as Mike went down on the boy; his tongue lapped at the peehole like a dog at its bowl and as gentle fingers pulled the foreskin back as far as it would go, lips followed down the rigid column engulfing the flesh until his nose buried itself in soft curly hair. Mike's right hand roamed over the smooth flat stomach while the left wandered over the delicate ball sack and then further between the parted thighs.

Brad was becoming restless, the excitement tuning up every nerve in his body to bursting point; he tried desperately to control himself but when a finger touched his hole, his cock spewed another litre of warm milk down Mike's throat.

"I'm sorry, Mike, I can't stop it!"

"Don't apologise, just think of all the fun you've been missing during your teenage years. Now, lay on your side and bring your knees close to your chest." Mike smeared some cool jelly around the virgin hole and a lot more along his protected stem. "Just relax as my finger penetrates your hole." The man lied as he eased forward pushing his wet and slippery cock into the prepared cave, "relax and it won't hurt." Mike had broken the barrier and was sliding through the unexplored tunnel until he was all the way in; he gradually pulled almost out then repeated the process increasing the speed with every thrust. Mike pushed his hand under the boy's waist and held the steel-hard cock and began jerking it to and fro. This encouraged the boy to clench his bum muscles together stimulating the already thrilling feeling around Mike's cock.

Bradley couldn't believe the fantastic sensation he was receiving from the stranger and knew he was only seconds away from messing up the sheets and as he came he tightened his cheeks so much Mike had no option but to cum. He extracted his weakening cock from the warm passage and discarded the condom into a plastic bag.

"I hope you enjoyed it as much as I did, Bradley."

"That was fantastic, nothing like that has ever happened to me before, thanks Mike, but I will always wonder what it would have felt like if you'd put your cock up my bum instead of your finger!" They both laughed.

Chapter 2

BRAD OPENED HIS EYES and wondered where he was, his head hurt like the worst hangover ever, his vision was blurred and he didn't recognise his surroundings.

"You're awake then?" A young voice called.

The room had bars like a prison cell, Brad was completely disorientated, he was naked and when he touched himself his body hair had disappeared. He squinted into the half-light to see where the voice had come from.

"Over here, on the other side of the room, man, am I glad to see someone else!"

"What am I doing here? Am I in prison?"

"Sort of, the guy upstairs brought you here a few hours ago. It's like a big garage or something under the house"

"Why? What's going on?"

"I don't know what you did but I was up the mountain and missed my bus, this guy, Mike he calls himself, stopped and offered me a lift, that was weeks ago. I've been here since."

"I've got to get out of here, there are people who will be looking for me!"

"Well, I hope you have better luck than me, I was at my wits ends thinking of ways to escape when I first arrived."

"Does he feed you?"

"Chinese three times a day, I've probably got slanted eyes by now."

Brad's own eyes were focusing again and the image speaking to him came into view. The boy had short cropped hair, high cheek bones and a handsome face, he was muscular and looked fit but the one thing that caught his eye was the all over suntan. "My head is spinning, I can't think straight." A sudden noise made the nervous youth jump.

"That will be the shutters opening, mind your eyes the sun is low in the sky and it's quite dazzling. By the way, my name's Martin, if I could reach I would shake your hand or your cock if you'd prefer." He giggled.

"You sound too happy to be a prisoner, why is that?"

"I had a boring life back in England, boring job, boring friends and very boring cold, rainy weather; then I came to Tenerife for a holiday, got lost and ended up here. The guy upstairs looks after all my comforts; apart from feeding me he performs the most fantastic things imaginable on my body, just thinking about them makes my cock go hard, look!"

As the shutters fully opened the whole room was bathed in sunlight and Brad could see Martin's hairless cock pointing towards the ceiling. He felt a stirring in his ball bag and turned away in case the boy had seen it move. A double metallic sound released the two cell doors and Martin stepped out standing in the warm early morning sun. A hatch in the wall raised and two trays of food and orange juice appeared.

"You see, it's not all bad!" Martin smiled showing two rows of sparkling white teeth, "oh yes, the bathroom is through that door!" He took his tray and sat on some long cushions spread out on the floor; Brad joined him and they ate breakfast together in the sun. "Give me your tray and I'll take it back to the hole in the wall then I'll put some sun cream on you, it might be January in England but it's like a hot day in July here."

Happy Martin poured some cream into his hands and began spreading it over Brad's pale skin. "Your body is really soft," he spoke quietly as he rubbed the sweet-smelling lotion into Brad's neck and shoulders, "lay on your stomach and I'll do your back." Brad complied with the instruction and felt the soothing fingers pressing into his flesh; it was like having a massage.

The top half was coated with the sun shield and Martin commenced the treatment on the feet and legs, Brad's sturdy thighs needed a lot of attention but not as much as his arse cheeks! Martin positioned himself between Brad's wide open legs and dug his fingers into the soft flesh then pulled the two mounds apart exposing the hole, "I'll put some in here to keep it nice and moist; it doesn't hurt to be prepared."

Bradley closed his eyes as the gentle fingers slowly probed his most secret place, the soothing cream felt cool and his rock-hard cock pressed against his stomach as he remembered what Mike had done to him last night. "Would you mind putting your cock in there?" He mumbled.

"You don't have to be so polite, Brad. If you want me to fuck you then say so!" He giggled again. Martin forced his iron rod away from his belly and pointed it towards the creamy hole, then drove home. "I think Mike has been here already, I've never seen a cock as big as his; I can tell you, it certainly made my eyes water the first time he did it to me."

"Had you done it before with anyone else?"

"Oh yes, many times, too many times! I was about twelve-years-old the first time but that's another story, how old were you on your first time?"

"My first time was with Mike last night."

Martin stopped pumping, taking his weight on his arms. "You were a virgin until last night? Wow, I'll have to order a bottle of champagne with our meal tonight!" He giggled once more before continuing with the action.

Five minutes passed, Martin had been quiet for five whole minutes, only now was he panting, Brad could feel the sweat dripping from the body above as the cock raced to and fro inside him, "I'm coming Brad, oh Jesus that feels so good!" The long thick weapon was slowly withdrawn and Martin sat back on his knees. "You'd better turn over, big boy, and let me do something to you." Brad turned onto his back exposing his enormous length. "Now, that's what I call a cock, you must have had a lot of boyfriends and lovers in your life."

"No, none, I told you, Mike was the first!"

"Well then allow me to be the second person to enjoy your lovely piece of flesh."

"Go slowly otherwise I'll come!"

"That's the idea of doing it, my dear!"

Bradley had only felt Mike's mouth around his cock, but the sensation he was feeling from Martin's was ten times greater, within seconds he was writhing around on the floor and moaning loudly as the warm tongue licked around and under his throbbing crown. Martin's gentle fingers held the stem, moving it slowly up and down, then the lips tightened and began sliding down the shaft until the helmet lodged in his throat and that's when Brad came. Poor Martin coughed and spluttered as the juice poured down his windpipe; he was unable to speak for at least another five more minutes!

"You tried to drown me!"

"I tried to warn you, I've been storing the stuff up for years and now the tap's been opened I can't switch it off." It was Bradley's turn to laugh.

Brad walked to the window and received a shock, the drop was sheer, maybe a hundred feet or more; he'd never had a good head for heights and stepped back. "I can see why you said escape would be difficult."

"You'd need wings to get out of this place but as I said before, I'm in no hurry to leave and now you're here I think I might want to stay forever!" Martin ran his hand over Brad's firm bum. "Let me put some cream on this side before the sun burns you." His other hand wandered over Brad's chest.

Bradley lay back down on the cushions, "why did Mike shave us?"

"He didn't shave us, that's a special cream he uses, the hair never grows back again; look, he did mine weeks ago and it's as smooth as a baby's bum, you can touch it if you want to." Bradley ran his fingers over Martin's soft skin around his cock and under his balls. "Can I suck yours?"

"I thought you'd never ask. Come on, change places." Martin spread eagled himself and closed his eyes.

Brad gazed down at the loose flesh lying across the flat stomach unsure where to touch first. He lifted the cock and was surprised how heavy it was, he began stroking it as if he had a small animal in his hands and it began to expand. As the stem grew, the petals slid back exposing the beautiful bloom; he examined it closer witnessing the pollen seeping from the peehole. His tongue licked at the bitter-sweet juice, the column twitched and he gently squeezed the swollen crown until more of the sap appeared. Using his thumb and forefinger he spread the oil-like substance over and under the pulsing head. His lips then covered the pink flower, his tongue moving rapidly sideways cleaning away the pollen before descending down the stem. The root was too far away for his mouth but his hands roamed over the hairless area, touching and feeling. Bradley was on cloud nine with the boy's cock deep inside his mouth and was in no rush to finish; his slow up and down action was there to give pleasure to the youth, not gratification for himself.

The silence in the prison was broken by the food hatch being opened and closed but neither was hungry for Chinese cuisine, their sexual appetite had not yet been fulfilled.

The light touch of Martin's hands gently caressed Bradley's head without forcing him down. Nobody had ever given him such a satisfying blow-job and although he'd been on the brink of cuming he'd managed to control himself but not for much longer; fingers had crept between his strong thighs and were approaching his weakness. The hole was tickled very slowly and gradually the digit moved inside, "Oh Jesus, Brad, I'm coming."

The thick cream hit the roof of Bradley's mouth and he began swallowing until the spray ceased, but he kept the hard flesh between his lips squeezing the last drops of semen out of the tube. He lifted his head and gazed down at the contented face. "I thought you were going to put some sun cream on me!" They both laughed.

After eating the cold food and drinking the warm orange, Martin finally spread the lotion over Bradley and for the next few hours they laid under the hot sun. "Time to turn over my love!" Martin said to his new friend.

"Am I really your love?"

"You could be if we're down here for another ten years." He giggled.

"But neither of us will be young in another ten years, we'll both be past our sell-by date, then what will happen to us. It's a long way down via the window; there may be broken bones down there already!"

"Stop it Brad, you're scaring me."

"When Mike plays around with you, is it down here or upstairs?"

"Up on his bed, why?"

"Couldn't you attempt to escape then if you wanted to?"

"Hardly, he's got these strong rubber handcuffs he puts on me, besides where would I go, this place is in the middle of nowhere. There's no telephone either and we're out of range for a mobile up here, I know that 'cause I tried mine when I first got here."

"But there'll be two of us, perhaps we could overpower him and take his truck."

"Perhaps, let's wait and see."

Michael Young had seen and heard everything on his closed circuit television, Martin had not been a problem but he would have to tread carefully as far as Bradley was concerned, he was a strong little fucker . . .

Chapter 3

BRAD TOOK A SHOWER and was followed into the cubicle by Martin; they smothered each other in bubbles and foam and when Brad looked at his reflection in the mirror he could see his hairless region but not only the patch above his cock had been deprived of hair; on closer inspection his arms, legs, chest, armpits, ball-bag and even his arse was as it had been before his teen years. His head was the only place left with any hair! He smiled at himself and what he saw pleased him!

The silence was broken by metallic shutters dropping, blocking out the setting sun and turning day into night. Warm air blowing through a vent in the wall kept the temperature stable; at this altitude it could became quite cool at night. The hatch opened and the two earlier trays were replaced with fresh hot food from Asia; there was no orange juice!

It was maybe an hour later when the key turned in the lock and Mike's voice ordered them back into their own cells. "Stay away from the doors, they close automatically."

"Why have you brought us here? What do you intend doing with us?" Brad was anxious to know.

"You are here to enjoy yourself. Tell me this; would you have had so much fun if you had been with your mates getting pissed up in the night clubs? You would most likely have stayed in bed all day and then done the same thing all over again. Even in this poor light I can see you've benefited from the sun's rays already. Martin is quite happy to stay with me and I'm sure after a while you will feel the same. Think of it as company for a middle aged man."

"But you are holding us against our will, that's kidnapping . . ."

"Now, now, settle down, why don't the three of us go upstairs and crack open a bottle of wine and enjoy ourselves for half an hour."

Bradley knew it was useless trying to reason with a man holding all the trump cards, besides he had learned a lot from Mike last night and he hadn't been forced to do anything he didn't want to. "Martin say's we have to wear handcuffs, is that really necessary?"

"You'll see why later, put your hands behind your back, please."

They really were made of a soft rubber but as Brad flexed his strong arms he could feel they were not made to be broken. Martin was cuffed in the same manner and the three of them trooped up the stairs to Mike's bedroom where they sat on the wide bed, the same bed that served to educate Brad last night.

"What have you got planned, Mike?" Martin was keen to know.

"We'll have a drink of my homemade brew first, it helps me relax." He undid one side of Martin's handcuffs reattaching it to the bedstead giving the boy a free hand to drink the wine. Then did the same to Bradley, this could be his chance to escape but he put the idea out of his head, he wanted to learn more of the games Mike and Martin played.

Two glasses of the cool refreshing drink had Martin giggling as Mike removed his dressing gown revealing his enormous cock.

"If you've finished your drink Bradley, we'll commence with the night's entertainment." Another set of handcuffs were used to clamp Brad's wrist to the other side of the bed and yet more secured his ankles; he was anchored on four corners! "We'll cover your eyes with this mask, it makes it more exciting." Bradley didn't object.

He felt hands dancing along his arms and under his armpits, then over his chest and down towards his stomach, the two pairs of hands were in unison floating over his skin with the pressure of butterflies landing on leaves; his body was responding to the delicate tickling touch, he began squirming on the bed, his head turning from side to side, but most noticeable was his steel hard cock pulsating against his stomach! His recently de-furred balls were next to receive the tender touch, two sets of fingers gently pinched and squeezed the bag while another pair stroked the inside of Brad's thighs driving him into a frenzy. From his crotch to his ankles the slow stroking sensation had the boy raising his buttocks from the bed, he was in ecstasy and still his cock throbbed waiting for a hand or mouth to relieve the pressure but neither did! Lips settled on Brad's mouth and a tongue reached inside touching his; the passionate embrace allowed him to relax his tense body before the next surprise. He felt someone climb over him, their knees either side of his chest and as the mouth left his it was replaced by the head of a cock; he licked at the moisture seeping from the eye, then as he opened his mouth wider the bulbous head disappeared inside to be tasted and slavered. He gripped tightly with his lips as the wide flesh slipped in and out, then the roaming hands found his spiky nipples and between finger and thumb gently twisted; Brad moaned with the cock still wedged firmly in his mouth and then a finger began tantalising his hole. Very slowly it traced a circle around the opening before pushing inside; Brad began panting hard and then erupted!

Martin felt the full force of the powerful jets of cum as they sped up the tube to freedom hitting him on the back in quick succession; it was game over! The mask was removed and the cuffs untied; Brad sat up with a smile on his face. "You won't need to cuff me anymore, if these are the games you play in the evenings I want to stay!

Chapter 4

A WEEK PASSED, BRAD'S plane left without him and he didn't care; he had found a sexual pleasure on the island he would never have even searched for on the cold streets of England. He'd become used to the Chinese food three times a day and noticed he was losing a few centimetres off his waistline. He kept himself fit by doing sit-ups and push-ups and like Martin, had an all over suntan. The cells were left unlocked at night encouraging the two youths to sleep together.

In the early morning of day eight there was a commotion; Mike was bringing a new boy into the secret room, it was obvious he'd been drugged and was mumbling incoherently; the man placed him in the spare cell and went back upstairs without saying a word.

"I thought he would have been satisfied with the two of us, why does he want anymore?" Martin whispered.

"Perhaps one of us has reached termination day and as you've been here the longest it will probably be you." Brad joked but Martin didn't think it funny.

"He likes me a lot more than you, he's frightened you'll do something to hurt him, he told me so!"

"He knows I'm happy here, I wouldn't hurt him anymore than I'd hurt you unless you want me to twist your nipples again!" He laughed then cuddled up to Martin resting his cock against the opening.

The new boy was awake and making a lot of noise. "Get me out of here!" He yelled.

"Go back to sleep," Martin called harshly, "we'll tell you why you're here when it's light!"

The new boy began whimpering, "Please let me out, I've done nothing wrong!"

Brad remembered what he'd felt like that first morning, waking up in a strange and sinister place. He untangled himself from Martin and spoke through he bars of the new boy's cage.

"What's your name?"

"Jim Carter." He spoke softly with a tremor in his voice.

"Ok, we'll call you Jimmy." Brad smiled but as it was as black as coal in the room it probably went unnoticed, "it's my guess you met a guy called Mike and both of you had some fun and games. Mike must like you a lot and wants you to play with him some more, that's why we are here, I'm Brad and the one with the squeaky voice is Martin." He laughed.

"I haven't got a squeaky voice, I'm butch!"

"How long will he keep me here?"

"Well, I've been here for over a week and Butch has been here for a month or more, it's not so bad if you like Chinese food and plenty of sunshine but if you have someone waiting for you back in England then you will probably be homesick."

"There's nobody waiting for me," he began to sob, "the day I left to come on holiday I told my parents I was gay. I'd met a man who said he loved me, we booked the holiday to Tenerife then the day we were leaving he sent me a text message saying he'd found somebody else."

Martin joined Brad at the cage. "What did your mum and dad say when you told them?"

"They told me not to bother coming back!"

Brad reached through the bars and touched Jimmy's warm shoulder, "how did you meet up with Mike?"

"I got a taxi from the airport to the hotel we'd booked into and found the reservation had been cancelled, I sat in the little bar next door not knowing what to do next; that's when Mike walked in and bought me a drink. One thing led to another and he offered to put me up for a couple of nights."

Brad could understand his dilemma; it wasn't too far away from what happened to him. "Don't worry we'll look after you."

"And be prepared for a shock when daylight comes, Mike has probably removed your body hair." Squeaky voice added with a giggle.

"You're right, he has!"

Chapter 5

THE SHUTTERS LIFTED BATHING the room in sunlight, Brad stepped carefully over sleeping Martin to see how the new boy was coping; Jimmy was uncovered, curled up into a ball with one hand through the bars. Brad laid on the warm floor watching the pretty face of the tormented boy then touched the cupped hand, the soft skin showed little signs of manual labour and nails were well manicured and clean. As Jimmy opened his eyes Brad increased his grip and smiled. "I thought you might want to see a friendly face when you woke up."

"You're Brad, I recognise your voice."

"And I am the beautiful Martin," Butch pirouetted in the middle of the floor bringing a smile to the new boy's face, "and if you call me squeaky voice again, Bradley, I will chew your balls off one at the time and very slowly!"

Jimmy stood up covering his shyness with his hands. "Where are my clothes?"

"You don't wear clothes any more, my dear, we are part of a new breed that just lets it all hang or you can be like Brad who walks around all day with a permanent hard-on!" Jimmy's cell door opened automatically and the hatch lifted for breakfast. "I wonder what surprise awaits us this morning, well I never, it's rice with more rice!" Camp Martin announced.

Brad eyed the newcomer up and down, in fact he couldn't take his eyes off him! For someone who had never been so much as fond of anyone before, he found himself attracted like a magnet to Jimmy. Maybe it was his bright blue eyes, his boyish face or perhaps his sturdy body . . .

Jimmy was aware of the attention he was getting and smiled at his admirer, Brad lost control of his emotions, walked up to Jimmy and wrapped his arms around the surprised boy. "You are the most gorgeous creature God ever made," he whispered before planting a kiss on the boy's soft lips. Jimmy returned the hug, digging his nails into Brad's back; he too needed to feel the comfort of another's body.

"Did I miss something? Perhaps I should change my deodorant!" Martin stood with hands on hips watching the pair kissing and cuddling like they had known each other for years.

The door opened and Mike beckoned to Martin, "can you drive?" He asked quietly.

"Yes, I have a Volkswagen Beetle back home but I expect the battery will be flat by now, and the tyres, if some vandal hasn't stolen them already . . ."

"OK, Martin, settle down, I want you to drive me to the hospital, I'm not feeling well, come upstairs and put your clothes on."

Brad was aware of Martin's hasty retreat with Mike but took no notice; he was too occupied with the boy in his arms! He and Jimmy sank to the floor without separating their lips, hands began roaming over each other, touching, feeling and gripping wherever there was flesh. "I think I'm in love!" Brad panted as their lips separated. Jimmy smiled and reached for Brad's super-stiff cock prising it away from his belly, "your hands are so soft and cool, but I must warn you I do cum very fast!"

The new boy turned around pointing his own cock into Brad's face; both mouths opened simultaneously and engulfed the other's crown.

Jimmy had only done this once before, it was on the guy who let him down the day before his holiday; maybe he hadn't done it right, perhaps that was the reason for the split. He was going to put as much love into sucking Brad's cock as he could!

His mouth gripped tightly around the silky skin sliding up and down on the pulsating rod while his tongue darted swiftly over the veined gland and all the time fingers crept over sensitive skin edging their way between Brad's powerful thighs, he heard moans and was aware of Brad panting but continued with the mouth action and finger probing until he felt the first of several gushes of sperm flood into his throat. This was a first for Jimmy and without a thought emptied his own tube into Brad's accommodating mouth. Two sweating bodies sat up and smiled at each other.

Brad looked deeply into Jimmy's eyes "I really do think I'm in love with you!"

"I've never believed in love at first sight, but when you spoke to me in the darkness last night you were so compassionate and caring, I couldn't wait to see what you looked like. You are the most handsome person I've ever seen and I reckon I could spend the rest of my life with you."

They showered, smothered each other in kisses and sun cream then spent the day changing colour. It was late in the afternoon when the door opened and a tearful Martin sat on the floor in front of the two new lovers.

"What's the matter, you look frightened?" Brad stood up and wrapped his comforting arms around camp Martin's shoulders.

"Mike's been told he's got a major problem with his heart!" He began sobbing, "they've kept him in the hospital to do tests; it doesn't look good for him. I've come back to get some things he needs."

Brad placed his hands on either side of the sorrowful boy's face, using his thumbs to wipe away the tears, "you're in no fit state to drive; you'll have an accident and end up in hospital yourself! We'll all go, it'll do us good to get a change of scenery."

Martin showed the boys where their clothes had been stored and while they were dressing he grabbed the items Mike had requested, placing them in a holdall. Brad was thrilled to get behind the wheel again but Martin was not a good passenger and kept talking nervously all the way to town. Jimmy sat in silence behind the driver watching the countryside fly passed and reminiscing in his mind the passionate lovemaking he and Brad had enjoyed earlier.

The receptionist at the private hospital spoke good English and directed them to the ward allowing them ten minutes and no excitement. Pipes, tubes and screens surrounded the bed monitoring the ashen-faced invalid who had aged by twenty years; Martin bent down and kissed his cheek.

Mike opened his eyes and without moving his head gazed at three solemn faces staring at him, "I'm not dead yet! A smile would be nice."

"What did the doctor say?" Brad asked taking hold of the hand without a needle in it.

"He told me I've got a blockage and they are going to operate on me in the morning, but I expect you'll all be gone back to England by then." He was more than a little grumpy.

Brad smiled and gripped tighter on the trembling hand. "We're not going anywhere, in fact we are going to look after you until you've had enough of us!" He leaned forward and kissed Mike's forehead. "If it wasn't for you, I would still be the naïve teenager without love but you have introduced me to a world of pleasure and now I've met Jimmy I don't think I'll ever want to go home."

A tear ran down Mike's cheek as his eyes shifted between Brad and his new friend, "Will you keep my plants watered . . ."

The door suddenly opened and a smartly dressed nurse indicted the boys should leave. Martin ensured the sick man he would take care of everything then kissed his cheek again. As soon as they sat in the pick-up Martin began snivelling again. "He's going to die, I know he is!"

"If the doctor thought that he wouldn't be operating on him tomorrow, would he?" Brad told him, "just relax and stop worrying!"

"Any chance of getting something to eat, I'm starving!" Jimmy alerted them to the fact they hadn't eaten since breakfast and it was late afternoon.

Brad reached into his trouser pocket and retrieved a fifty-euro note. "I'd almost forgotten I had this, let's find a restaurant!"

Three well-fed teenagers drove back up into the hills just before darkness fell. Martin began watering the greenery while Brad and Jimmy cleaned and tidied their new home. "Look what I found in the fridge!" Brad held up a bottle of Mike's special brew then poured three glasses. "Here's to Mike's speedy recovery!" They touched glasses and swallowed the contents.

"I think I'll sleep in Mike's bed tonight," Martin began, "it will make me feel closer to him."

"How about if all three of us sleep in Mike's bed." Jimmy suggested. "I still feel I've a lot to learn."

"That's a great idea and it will stop you worrying, Martin. Last one to become naked gets a spanking."

Martin took his usual stance with hands on hips, "in that case I'm definitely in no hurry!" All three laughed.

The two new lovers watched each other peel out of their clothes and as soon as Brad dropped his boxers, his cock slapped hard against his stomach. A wide smile spread across Jimmy's pretty face before he fell to his knees and began licking the straining column.

"I hope I'm included in your love making," Martin remarked as he lay on his back pulling on his seven inches. Brad and Jimmy jumped onto the bed then took it in turns sucking on Martin's pole until he yelled with pleasure, coming in Jimmy's mouth.

Brad whispered into Martin's ear, then squeaky voice reached under the bed and produced the rubber handcuffs. "You'll enjoy this Jimmy." Brad secured his new friend's wrists and ankles to the four corners then blindfolded him.

"Are you going to hurt me?"

"Only if you want us to!" Squeaky voice laughed. The tormenting fingers soon had Jimmy writhing on the bed and Brad almost came as he watched his new friend's bulging muscles flexing in an attempt to free his tethered limbs.

"Relax and enjoy, Jimmy!" Brad whispered and in an instant, a calmness overcame the youth. Martin climbed from the bed and opened a drawer then pointing a finger to his lips to indicate silence produced a massive rubber cock. He drenched the length in lubricant then smeared more of the same around Jimmy's hole.

"If you find my cock too big for you then holler!" Martin giggled as he gently inserted the huge probe. Jimmy's blindfolded face contorted and his body seemed to lift from the bed as the imitation cock penetrated deeper until it could go no further. Brad pinched Jimmy's nipples making him moan with pleasure while Martin slowly moved the artificial cock to and fro.

"Is that all you've got, Martin?" Jimmy said seriously and we started laughing hilariously. Brad removed the mask and squeaky voice pulled out the slippery cock holding it up for Jimmy to see.

"Jesus! I'll never be able to walk with my legs together again." He laughed as his handcuffs were removed.

Chapter 6

W<small>HEN</small> B<small>RAD</small> <small>OPENED</small> <small>HIS</small> eyes the sun was already high in the sky. Jimmy's warm body was close to his but there was no sign of Martin in the wide bed. Brad tried unsuccessfully to extricate himself from the arms of his sleeping friend. "Where are you going?" Jimmy asked through half open eyes.

"To look for Martin!"

"I'll come with you, I need a piss anyway."

Squeaky voice was nowhere in the house but they could hear singing coming from the garden. Martin was prancing in all his nakedness over the green foliage with hosepipe in hand spraying the wilting plants. "You seem to have found your purpose in life!" Brad shouted and as he did so the powerful water jet hit him full in the chest. He jumped to the next row of plants avoiding the cold, powerful shower and dived for Martin's legs knocking him to the ground. The hosepipe went on a crazy route soaking them both before finally being retrieved by Jimmy who was out of his mind with laughter. The muddy ground covered the two youths and Jimmy volunteered to wash them clean but instead of using the hose he began pissing over them. Within seconds all three were squirming in the slippery piss-soaked soil.

When normality returned they hosed each other clean before entering the house. It was getting close to midday and Martin suggested they make their way to the hospital. "He should be out of the theatre by now."

"Don't look so worried, he'll want to see happy, smiling faces when he opens his eyes, not gloomy ones." Brad wasn't sure himself what the outcome of the heart surgery would be. Even if Mike survived he may need special care that he and the other two couldn't provide.

The long drive to the hospital gave all three time to reflect on the time spent at the house, there had been a change in their lives and not one of them regretted being taken from their dull and mundane existence. They discussed the curious meeting with Mike that had brought three lonely souls together and made a pact that whatever the outcome they would look after him.

The nurse smiled as she looked at three anxious faces approaching the ward. "He's fine; the surgeon unblocked an artery that was causing the problem. You can take him home later today but remember; he must do no heavy lifting, needs plenty of rest and most importantly, don't let him get excited for at least a week!"

"That won't be easy." Martin giggled.

Mike was sitting up in bed reading a newspaper when they entered. "I've been told I should be OK for another twenty years or so." He said in a matter-of-fact manner without looking up.

"First of all, we're glad you've made a good recovery. Secondly, the three of us have made a decision, we will stay with you until you've had enough of us, unless of course, you've got some pretty nurse lined up." Brad smiled.

Mike dropped his paper and looked at three grinning faces, "I thought you would have taken advantage of the situation to make your escape, denounce me to the police for kidnapping then flee back to England."

"But if we did that you'd have nobody to do this for you," Martin slid his hand under the sheet and wrapped his long slender fingers around the expanding flesh.

"Hey! Didn't the nurse say no excitement?" Jimmy chipped in and all four laughed.

The End